What the critics are saying:

"As hot as volcanic lava is the only way to describe Rhyannon Byrd's first release, Waiting For It...Her characters are wonderful arousing and full of heart...Jake and Taylor erupt like a volcano, burn everything they touch and keep the reader coming back for more...Rhyannon Byrd is a new author to erotic fiction and already a name on my must buy list. Don't sit around waiting for this one to come to you. Go and get it quickly, it's a tale not to be missed." ~*Tracey West, The Road to Romance*

"**Waiting For It** is an intensely erotic and emotional book...If you enjoy highly erotic contemporary stories, with a heavy dose of emotion thrown in and a beautiful HEA (happily ever after) ending to top it off, give **Waiting For It** a try. This title belongs in my 'keeper' shelf."

~*Mireya, A Romance Review*

D1430751

Discover for yourself why readers can't get enough of the multiple award-winning publisher Ellora's Cave. Whether you prefer e-books or paperbacks, be sure to visit EC on the web at www.ellorascave.com for an erotic reading experience that will leave you breathless.

www.ellorascave.com

WAITING FOR IT
An Ellora's Cave Publication, July 2004

Ellora's Cave Publishing, Inc.
PO Box 787
Hudson, OH 44236-0787

ISBN #1-4199-5004-5

ISBN MS Reader (LIT) ISBN # 1-84360-849-9
Other available formats (no ISBNs are assigned):
Adobe (PDF), Rocketbook (RB), Mobipocket (PRC) & HTML

Edited by *Pamela Campbell*.
Cover art by *Darrell King*.

WAITING FOR IT

Rhyannon Byrd

Chapter 1

The woman behind the counter had the largest set of breasts Taylor had ever seen. They swayed with an endless jiggle, requiring a marvel of engineering to keep them contained—which she obviously didn't possess. The tiny pink buttons on her uniform barely held her in as she flashed her most malicious smile. It was all teeth and red smeared lips the locals all claimed had been packed full of collagen.

Taylor felt a little sick every time she saw them.

Not with jealousy. Not of Wanda Merton. No, it was just the image of those crimson colored things wrapped around her ex-husband's cock that made her queasy as hell. It'd been over a year now, but she could still see the two of them writhing across her bed as if it had been only yesterday.

There were just some things a woman could never forget. Taylor assumed finding your husband in bed with the town whore must be one of them. Everyone in Westin knew Mitch had screwed around on her, but it was finding the two of them in her own bed that had finally given her the motivation to kiss his sorry ass goodbye.

She'd stayed married to the miserable jerk for seven years—seven years too long in her estimation. And that was never as obvious as when she came face-to-face with Mason's Groceries' checkout clerk.

"Bet you didn't know Jake Farrell's back in town," Wanda sneered, hitching her beefy hip against the register. "Tucker over at the Gas and Dash said he just filled up a shiny new truck 'bout twenty minutes ago."

For a split second, Taylor's heart stopped. It hung heavily in her chest, a tight ball of warring confusion and lifelong desire, suspended in time. Then it kicked back in with a hearty vengeance, pumping blood through her thin frame in a dizzying rhythm. It was all she could do to hide her stunned reaction from the cruel bitch who was supposed to be ringing up her juice and eggs.

Trying to sound unaffected, Taylor struggled to make a casual reply. "Jake Farrell back in Westin? I wonder what on earth could've brought him back to this place."

"Aw, I don't know," Wanda drawled, smacking her lips around a huge, nauseating wad of grape-colored bubble gum. "Maybe he just came back to rub your snotty nose in the dirt some more? Never was anythin' more entertainin' back in school than listenin' to Mitch tell everybody the latest Jake had said about you. That guy musta hated your skinny ass somethin' fierce."

Something in Taylor's chest died a little at the spiteful words. Oh, she knew Jake hadn't liked her back when they were in school, but she'd never really understood why. He'd left the summer after he graduated and she hadn't seen him since. Not even her ex-husband Mitch—Jake's best friend—had heard from him in all that time.

As far as Taylor knew, no one in the whole town of Westin had ever set eyes on him again. He'd lived with an uncle who had moved over to Pressmore when he left—so all ties to Westin had been broken the moment he'd driven away.

After ten years, it seemed beyond crazy that she could still feel so wounded by the fact that Jake Farrell hadn't liked her, but she did. She'd tried to get beyond it—to forget him—but it killed her a bit more every time she thought about him.

As ridiculous as it was, she'd loved that gorgeous boy from the moment she'd first set eyes on him at the silly age of sixteen. She'd been mystified by the tall, dark-haired, green-eyed football player. Panting breath, damp palms, and red-faced every single time he'd looked at her. He was two years older, and back then—well, eighteen had seemed like a lifetime. He'd been the sinful, sexy, older man of her dreams and she'd never forgotten him.

Hah! Like she ever would. She'd spent the past ten years poring over all the delicious details of him imprinted in her memory, transforming them into life with her paint and brush.

Of course, it was going to be a cold day in hell before Taylor let Wanda Merton catch so much as a whiff of her interest in the man. Talk about inviting trouble. Not that it was anything but blatantly obvious to anyone with half a brain who'd ever seen her work, but then she doubted Wanda had ever lain hands on one of her books. If she had, it'd probably been to toss it on the floor and stomp on it with her two big feet.

Swiping her check card, Taylor managed to mumble, "Well, I'm sure you know more about him than I do."

In fact, she knew she did, and it was a memory she'd wasted what seemed like forever trying to forget.

Wanda knew it too, but it didn't stop a feral, Cheshire Cat smile from spreading slowly across her smug face. "Down to the last thick inch, Taylor Moore."

She tried, but she couldn't help it. She went absolutely breathless at the thought of Jake Farrell's long, thick inches.

"How, uh, lucky for you then, Wanda," she wheezed around the lump of lust in her throat, barely able to draw enough air.

Then there was no breath at all as a deep, smoky voice behind her rumbled, "I must be luckier than I thought to have found you so quickly."

Oh, Jesus.

Jake Farrell was standing at her back, the heat of his big body kissing the entire length of hers! His breath brushed the back of her neck through the heavy mass of her hair, sending chills racing across the surface of her skin. And when she looked down, his large, rugged hands were braced against the counter on either side of her, caging her in.

Holy ever-loving hell.

When she didn't move or make any attempt to respond, he leaned closer and she heard him say, "Taylor?"

Heaven help her. His lips actually brushed against her scalp that time. She could hear the question in his sexy voice.

She was going to have to do something, but what? What? In all the lovesick scenarios she'd concocted over the years, she'd never imagined this—having him standing at her back while Wanda Merton looked on with a vicious scowl on her sour face.

"Come on, Taylor Moore," Jake teased over the fierce pounding of his heart, praying he could put her at ease before she ran from him. He could sense her indecision—

her nervousness—while his senses ran wild in a chaotic, exhilarating jumble of need and lust and raging emotion. He was more than willing to chase after her if she made a break for it, but the fucking wait just might kill him.

Hell, it was all he could do not to toss her up on the checkout stand and bury himself in her sweet little body right then and there. "I know you haven't forgotten me that easily, honey. Stop playin' possum."

Taylor didn't know whether she wanted to laugh or cry. He'd used her maiden name. Did that mean he knew about the divorce? Knew she was single? Geez, did he even know she'd ever been married?

Ignoring Wanda, she turned slowly within the circle of his strong, tanned, muscled arms, her heart stuttering at her first look at the man who'd stolen her heart a decade ago.

God help her. Please. Jake Farrell was everything she'd remembered and more. And any second now she was going to melt into a big, sopping puddle of need on the scarred linoleum floor. "No, I haven't, um, forgotten you—Jake."

How could I ever forget you?

Jake smiled down at her, his dark green eyes moving over everything at once. He seemed to drink her in, consuming her like a beast craving blood after a lifetime of tasteless water.

His avid gaze touched her hair and the delicate, almost fragile features of her face, from her small nose and wide set sable eyes, to her finely arched brows and lush pink mouth. He even studied her ears and the long, glossy strands of her hair all the way down to where the curled tips lay against her small breasts.

Beneath his hot stare, Taylor remained trapped in the moment. She swallowed again at the suffocating desire and her nipples went rock hard, spiking against the thin fabric of her shirt.

"I don't believe it," he rasped, deep voice full of wonder. "You're even better than I remembered."

Better!

Better than what?

Taylor didn't know what she might've said to the strange comment, but Wanda suddenly gasped behind her, rearing her ugly head.

"What are you doin' wastin' your time with this little runt, Jake? Everyone round here knows how much you've always hated her."

Jake answered the vindictive woman without ever taking his eyes from Taylor's. "Wanda, for once in your bitter life, why don't you try minding your own business?"

"What's got up your ass, Jake?" she sneered, raising her hackles like a she-cat preparing to swipe her claws. "You used to know how to give a woman a good time. What are you throwin' it away on her for now? Mitch's told everybody in town she's drier than sawdust." Her pouting lips sneered like a sick rendition of a reptilian smile, cruel and menacing. "Said it was like fuckin' a plank, sinkin' between her skinny spread legs."

Taylor had finally had enough. Well, she'd had enough about a decade ago, when she had first moved to town with her mother, but having to listen to Wanda put her down in front of Jake Farrell was too much even for her. She opened her mouth to say God only knew what, comebacks having never really been her strong point—at least not in the heat of the moment. Give her an hour and she'd be raring to go, the perfect blend of wit and scorn poised on the tip of her tongue. Of course, by that time, she was usually the only person left to impress.

Thankfully, Jake had no such problem with spontaneity.

"If Mitch never got her dripping," he drawled, "then it was his own pathetic fault for having a useless little prick. Something my uncle tells me you should know a lot about, Wanda. Didn't your Mama ever teach you not to fuck around with another woman's husband — even if he is the town sheriff?"

Wanda's face mottled the same crimson shade as her blusher, completing the clown-like effect of her makeup beneath the bright ruby sheen of her hair. "Feelin' jealous, Farrell? Mitch's got a lot to offer a woman where it counts."

Taylor watched the most sinfully sexy man she'd ever known, the one whose image haunted her dreams and still woke her in the dead of night with her panties slick — her aching pussy gone warm and creamy — flash the woman behind her a taunting smile.

"You call that a lot, Wan? Next time you're pretending he can make you come with it — remember I've got a helluva lot more."

His attention shifted back to Taylor, not that it hadn't been on her all along. His big, rough hands tunneled into the sides of her hair, holding her face still as he lowered his mouth toward her quivering lips.

He wasn't finished putting Wanda Merton in her place, though, and Taylor could feel the heady warmth of his breath as he spoke.

"And when Taylor's taking every inch of me, she won't have to pretend. She's gonna come till she's sticky sweet and my ears are ringing from the screaming."

His intense gaze roamed over her face, sending a wave of pure heat to her already flushed features. Taylor knew she must look dumbstruck, staring up at him like a deer caught in the headlights. But there wasn't anything else she could do. She *was* dumbstruck, shocked straight down to her toes.

She really couldn't help herself. She'd been stunned mute by his presence and his bold, outrageous words. And they were only getting bolder.

Keep 'em coming, baby, her Jake-starved body demanded. *Just keep 'em coming.* There was a wild, rough ride of lust and want pounding through her veins that had been gaining momentum since the first time she'd ever set eyes on the man.

"And that's just the first time," Jake went on, the deep timbre of his voice doing all kinds of warm, wicked things to places deep inside of her. "After we take the edge off, it'll only get better. Creaming for me is gonna become Taylor's favorite pastime. All day and all night, she'll just come all over me—my fingers, my cock, my face. We're gonna be swimming in it, Wanda, and your and Mitch's sorry asses won't be crossing our minds even once."

Okay, she was not going to think about what he'd just said. No way in hell! At least until she got home. Then she'd savor every fantastic word, playing them over and over in her mind while she slipped her fingers between her thighs and struggled for release.

Then he moved closer, and Taylor thought he was finally going to kiss her, but he brushed his thumb across her lips instead. His gaze was transfixed, concentrated, as if he were comparing their shape and texture to a memory.

"So, if you'll excuse us," he groaned with a hungry smile, "we've got things to do."

His eyes burned on Taylor, promising to make the outrageous claim a reality. But no—he couldn't possibly be serious, could he? The "things" they needed to do couldn't really be each other, could they? She was just a—well, she was just Taylor, while he looked sexier than a man should ever be allowed.

Who would ever believe the hero and the misfit? She sure as hell couldn't.

And he'd only gotten better with time. She loved the crinkles at the corners of his gorgeous green eyes. Loved the grooves that bracketed his sinful mouth. Loved the sun-bronzed gold of his tan and the musky outdoors scent of his skin.

He held out his hand and she took it as if she'd done it a thousand times before, when in reality, this morning was one of the few times they'd ever even touched.

Jake pulled her along beside him, her groceries and Wanda Merton left behind—forgotten—and Taylor followed the man of her dreams through the door, out into the brilliant, blinding light of the sun.

Chapter 2

When they reached her Jeep parked at the curb, Taylor turned to face the man who'd been both the bane and blessing of her entire existence.

The sun glinted behind his broad shoulders, backlighting his magnificent body the way she painted her Faeries and Warlocks. The same slash of a mouth promised to be ruthless and unforgiving in the pursuit of pleasure. Long, lean muscles that molded the shape of his white T-shirt and worn-out Levi's. Tall, tan, and ruggedly—insanely—make-your-pussy-ache-just-to-look-at-him handsome.

And that damn hair. Not short, not long, but just shaggy enough to wrap your fingers in the glossy black locks and take him wherever you needed him. Wherever *she* needed him. Her breasts, her stubborn clitoris, and then lower, to where he could sink his tongue inside of her the way she'd always read a man could pleasure a woman, but had never experienced for herself.

God, it was so ironically pathetic. Here she'd spent seven years married to the Westin stud, and she still didn't have any experience outside of the boring old missionary position. And Wanda was right about the not coming part. A fact Mitch had thrown in her face in defense of why he'd screwed around with half the town.

"If I can't make you cream," he'd told her on countless occasions, "no one can, sugar."

Well, Taylor wasn't so sure about that. Just looking at Jake Farrell made her feel closer to that elusive O than she ever had before. She wanted to break open the silver belt buckle on the front of his jeans, rip open the buttons of his fly, and sink her hand inside to explore the heavy bulge she'd seen there out of the corner of her eye as they'd walked outside. He wasn't actually hard yet, just beautifully full, as if he always nicely filled out the front of his pants.

And he did. He always had, even as a young man. Every girl he'd ever dated had said he had the biggest— equipment they'd ever seen. Massive, the rumors had told. Long and thick, and he knew a thousand different ways to make a woman scream with it.

Man oh man oh man.

Oh no. Suddenly Taylor realized just what she was doing. Here she was, standing in front of Mason's Groceries—staring at Jake Farrell's crotch! And God help her, she didn't know how long her eyes had been glued to that particular part of his anatomy, but it was growing bigger by the second.

Her heartbeat, which was already doing double-time, nearly flew right out of her chest. No, no, no! This was so incredibly embarrassing. Damn the blasted man and this sex-crazed feeling he'd always made her feel, even when he could've been halfway around the world for all she knew.

It was obvious she needed to say something, and she really needed to pull her fascinated stare away from his fly before she started to drool, but her treacherous body parts just weren't listening to reason.

Jake finally helped by tipping her face up with the side of his fist, forcing her to meet his glittering green gaze. Oh, he knew exactly what she'd been thinking about, she realized with a horrified groan. Taylor knew he could read it written all over her flushed face, as easy as a book.

"You okay, Taylor?"

He wasn't exactly smiling, but she could hear a hint of humor behind the deep, rough edge of his voice. Not to mention arousal and concern. His calloused thumb stroked lazily against her chin, caressing her flesh, the gentle touch unbearably arousing.

What on earth was going on? Jake Farrell back in town, acting like he actually wanted her? Nothing so strange or bizarre or unbelievably wonderful had ever happened in her entire life.

"Uh, yes, thank you. I mean I'm, um, fine."

And an idiot. I'm a complete, ridiculous, sex-starved idiot!

He nodded, his penetrating gaze seeing straight into her, as if he could find out all her secrets with just a look. "I'm sorry if I got carried away back there, but I couldn't resist. Is she always like that?"

Taylor knew exactly what he meant, and she couldn't help but wonder what he thought of Wanda's "Bitch of the Year" attitude. It would absolutely kill her to have Jake Farrell pity her.

Pride made her try a small laugh that fell as flat as her chest. "Wanda? Don't worry about her. This was actually a good day between us. Quite civil really."

The sensual line of his lips hardened into a grim line, betraying his anger. "You mean it gets worse than that?

18

Why in the hell don't you deck her and get away from this hole-in-the-wall town?"

Because I might never have seen you again, she thought with a violent rush of longing—and in that moment, she knew it was true. That was why she'd stayed all these years. Why she'd faced down all the loneliness and humiliation and painful memories. She'd been waiting for Jake to come home—to come back to her—afraid that if she left, their paths might never cross again.

Well, once a fool, always a fool, she figured, knowing how this man had always felt about her. Nothing. That was what he'd always felt. Not a single thing.

But he wasn't looking like he felt nothing at the moment. No, he looked like he wanted to lay her out on the hood of her car and taste her from head to toe, lingering on all the good parts in between. She couldn't believe this was Jake. Couldn't believe he was actually standing before her—the real flesh and blood man—and not some heartbreaking figment of her imagination.

"Well, um, thanks for what you did and all. It was, uh, really nice of you to stick up for me in there."

He moved closer, just a hairsbreadth away from actually touching her trembling body with his own. "Is that what I was? Nice?"

One corner of his mouth lifted in a gorgeous little crooked grin, like he was almost embarrassed, and the memory of it nearly floored her. It was the same expression she'd seen him wear back when people would stop him in town and go on and on about his latest success on the high school football field. Mitch had eaten it up, but Jake had always seemed uncomfortable with the outlandish praise, which had endeared him to her even more.

And, oh man, was he tall. She felt so small next to him—so deliciously feminine. "Well, I, uh, mean it was nice to act like you, um, like you—"

Ugh! She knew she was rambling like a half-wit here, but she couldn't get the words out.

He moved closer, and this time his crotch nudged into her belly. Wow, she nearly swallowed her tongue. Then his hands went back into her hair, the same way they had inside the store, and her heart nearly stopped at the thought that now he might kiss her.

Yes! Right here! Right now! This very instant, please!

"I wasn't trying to be nice. I was trying to put that jealous—"

"Jealous? Wanda Merton's never been jealous a day in her life!"

His fingers tightened, thumbs moving at her temples in a slow, seductive touch that he probably thought would relax her, but had the complete opposite effect, making her want to just crawl all over him like a wild woman. Her hands fisted at her sides to keep from grabbing anything she wasn't supposed to touch. And damn it—that was probably all of him.

His face lowered, their noses nearly brushing, and from this close Taylor could see all the brilliant streaks of light green star-bursting through the darker jade of his eyes. They were so incredibly beautiful. When she got home, she was going to paint them so she wouldn't forget a single enthralling detail.

"She's always been jealous of you, Taylor. Just like all the other two-faced women in this town who hated you for being beautiful and smart and talented. Who hated the way every guy watched your little fuck-me body every time you walked by. Haven't you figured it out yet, after all this time? They're all spitting with jealousy. All but green with it, honey."

Jake watched her beautiful eyes go wide with shock at his words, her expression completely disbelieving.

"Jake, what are you talking about?" she laughed, the sound shaky and strained. "Just look at me. It really was sweet of you to pretend for Wanda's benefit, but you're the one who used to tell everybody I looked like a scrawny runt. Mitch said you didn't know how he could stomach being seen with me when we'd go out together."

Jake laughed too, but it was a dark, rough sound that touched a place deep inside of her—someplace that had never been touched before. "He said all that, did he?"

She nodded, at least as much as she could with his hands holding her head, his thumbs still circling her temples.

"And what if I told you everything he said was a lie, Taylor? Would you believe me? He used to give me piles of bullshit about you too. About how you thought I was stuck on myself and dumber than shit. But I'm not buying it anymore, sweetheart. What if I told you everything I said to Wanda was the truth, and that I've spent the last ten years of my life wanting it—craving it?"

His voice lowered, his forehead dropping forward to rest against her own. "What if I told you I've wanted to get inside your pants and fuck you from the second I set eyes on you in school? Hell, you were barely sixteen when I first saw you, and I still wanted to take you home with me and lay you out on my bed and shove my face between your legs, just eating you out for hours on end. I never even thought about doing that to a girl until I met you, Taylor."

She tried to say something, but all that came out was some sort of hoarse, choked whimper. A small, needy sound of hunger and disbelief. But she wanted to believe. Oh, man, did she ever.

Then he pressed his mouth against her own. Hot and sweet and electric, a sensual assault of textures and tastes, and she knew she was going to die. Right there in the middle of Lincoln Street, in front of Mason's Groceries, Taylor Moore was going to die from the rapturous ecstasy of being kissed by Jake Farrell. The heart stopping moment was going to happen any second now.

His lips molded hers, eating at them, but not pushing inside. Not yet. "You can believe me, Taylor. It's true," he whispered hotly against her mouth, unable to get enough of her intoxicating taste. It was the one flavor he'd always hungered for and never found in any other woman.

"Mitch was a lying bastard because he could see how much I wanted you and it drove him crazy," he rasped, rubbing his lips against hers, marveling at their silky petal softness. "Nearly as crazy as it drove me to think of you with him, letting him touch you and kiss you and fuck you the way I wanted — no, needed to."

What? "But he didn't. I mean — I never slept with him until after we were married, Jake. Not till after you were gone."

His head lifted, hands tightening to hold her in place. "You don't have to lie to me, Taylor. Mitch told me the two of you screwed like rabbits every chance you got. That you would ride him so hard he couldn't see straight!"

He looked angry now, and she couldn't find the air to finish explaining. "But I never slept with him. Not back then. Not when we were dating."

His high cheekbones were slashed with color, voice little more than a snarl. "I'm beginning to think there isn't a damn thing that miserable bastard didn't lie about."

Taylor shook her head in a frantic motion, trying to make him understand. She could feel the rage simmering just beneath the hot surface of his skin, his fingers trembling against her face — and everything within her longed to soothe him. She wanted to be the woman to wrap him up in her arms and gentle his anger, but this was neither the time nor place. And no matter how strongly she wished it otherwise, she wasn't his woman.

The streets were thankfully empty at this early hour, but soon everyone would be coming into town and she knew they'd draw a crowd. No one around here had ever expected to see Jake Farrell yelling at her about being — er, uh, ridden by Mitch.

No, wait. She was the one who'd supposedly done the riding.

Yeah, right.

Since she couldn't look away because of his hold on her, she closed her eyes instead, trying to regain at least a modicum of control. "Jake, what are we doing? This is crazy. I have to go, and I'm sure you have to get to whatever brought you back to town."

What had brought him back? Man, she really wanted to know.

Jake released his hold on her face, only to move his big hands to her shoulders, curling around the delicate slopes. His fingers slipped beneath the edges of her sleeveless shirt, smoothing over satiny skin that felt softer than silk. "I'll follow you home, then. We'll finish this there. My Uncle Mark told me you live in the old Tupelo place now."

Taylor nibbled on her full lower lip, looking adorably befuddled. The knot in his shaft doubled, thinking of the moment when she'd close those soft lips around the head of his cock and nibble on him instead. Aw, hell, he was gonna come in his pants if he didn't get inside her soon. And knowing it wasn't going to happen any time soon made him want to cry like a friggin' baby.

"Jake, you don't have to follow me home. I'll be fine. You can go on and do your thing. You don't have to worry about me."

He couldn't stop the wicked grin spreading across his face. "The only thing I'm worried about, Taylor, is how long you're going to make me wait before crawling into bed with me."

Heat was blazing from her face now, her expression so cute and wonderfully confused.

"Jake, what are you talking about?" Her hand lifted to her forehead, rubbing as if she had a sudden headache pounding there. "God, I'm not awake enough for this. What are you doing here? Did you come back just to drive me crazy? Is this some kind of game? A joke?"

His hands trailed down her sides to settle at her waist, and he loved the way he could bracket her slim curves with his big hands. Everything about this woman, all the things she'd always hated about herself, turned him on to the point of pain. It was just one of those primitive, testosterone things. Her slight curves and delicate features just made him want to go all caveman on her.

For years he'd fantasized about being the man to rip away her pristine façade, stripping away all those cool layers of self-control until she was writhing like a maddened animal beneath him. An insatiable little creature that demanded he make her cream and scream and fuck her till she couldn't even remember her name.

Whenever he'd thought of how sex should be, he'd always thought of Taylor. Hell, probably a minute hadn't gone by in the past ten years that he hadn't thought about wanting her. And God help her, he had a decade of raunchy, lust-filled fantasies saved up to spend inside of her.

When he'd first left town, he'd been young and angry and confused, and for a long time he'd been stupid enough to think he'd be able to screw this woman out of his system. But it'd never worked. He knew without bragging that he could make a woman very, very happy in bed, but every woman he'd ever known came up short when compared to Taylor Moore. There was a part of him, something deep inside that had always been locked away, saving itself for her, and no amount of mindless fucking had been able to release it.

It just wasn't ever going to be enough until it was Taylor beneath him, screaming his name, raking her slender nails down his back while he broke her open, pounding her through the mattress or wall or wherever the hell else she'd let him fuck her. How many times had he fantasized about spreading her legs and plowing into her, watching the entire thing, seeing his thick cock stretch her open, feeling her pussy suck him in?

It'd be a penetration that went deeper than her body, straight into her soul.

He wanted to be able to take her right now. Just carry her over to his truck, toss her up in the back seat, and make love to her till they were both too dead to move. And that was just for starters. Like he'd said, he had a lot of time to make up for, and the rest of his life to do it.

But she was still too skittish. He fought the urge to drag his hands down the slope of her spine until they rested on that perfect little heart-shaped ass he'd always loved, knowing she'd probably pass out on him. Her pupils were dilated and she wasn't breathing quite right, and he couldn't help but feel like an arrogant prick for loving the way she reacted to him so easily. He'd barely even touched her and already she looked as if she'd convulse with pleasure.

Taylor licked her lips and tasted Jake there. A strange wave of peace buffeted her body. It was so odd. She'd never been kissed by Jake Farrell before, and yet, he tasted so wonderfully familiar. Warm and sweet and delicious, as if he'd been made just for her.

"Why are you here?" she whispered, trapped within his glittering green gaze. There were promises there she didn't dare trust herself to believe. She couldn't do it, not if she didn't want to be left shattered when he walked back out of her life. But she was helpless to look away. "What do you want from me, Jake?"

To hell with it. A man could only take so much, and a desperate man even less. She squealed the instant his hands grabbed hold of her backside, pulling her up against the searing heat of his body. Perfect, he thought. They were going to be so fucking good together.

"I came back for this," he growled, kneading the firm, resilient muscles beneath his palms while grinding his cock against her mound. The feel of her was incredible.

Soft and sleek and beautiful. And his. One hundred percent, irrevocably, undeniably his. "I came back for you, Taylor."

"You're crazy," she groaned.

"No, sweetheart, I'm determined."

Chapter 3

Jake followed her to the old Victorian on the edge of town, replaying every word of their exchange through his mind. What was she thinking? He knew he needed to be careful—knew she didn't come anywhere close to trusting him yet. It was just so hard when he got near her, both literally and figuratively. This thing between them was stronger than ever, stronger than even he'd expected. But at least he'd been expecting it. Taylor must feel like she'd just been blindsided.

He pulled in behind her in the long driveway, taking in all the telling details of her home at once. It was picture perfect, like something from a fairy tale—dark green with salmon pink shutters, a lush garden and an explosion of vibrant flowers from one end of the house to the other. They spilled from huge wooden tubs, hung from moss-lined baskets, scenting the morning air with their heady perfume. He loved it. If the house weren't here in Westin, he'd move here to live with her in a heartbeat.

But there was no way in hell he was going to stay here, not with the likes of Mitch and Wanda and the rest of his gang clouding their happiness. Taylor deserved a new beginning, and he was willing to move heaven and earth to give it to her. Hell, he could relocate his business to wherever she wanted, and when they got there, he'd build her a perfect replica of this place, right down to the Victorian eaves and cobblestone walkway.

With his body thrumming with anticipation and his cock all but crying to get at her, Jake climbed out of his F350. Taylor shot him a shy smile as she opened the front door, and he followed her through the dim, lemon-scented rooms back to the kitchen. She motioned for him to take a chair at the table, but stayed standing herself, putting the entire distance of the world between them.

She shifted uncomfortably, folding and unfolding her arms around her slim waist as if she wasn't quite sure what to do with them. Maybe she was itching to grab him as badly as he wanted to grab hold of her and toss her up on the gleaming pinewood table. God, he could only hope so. Then he'd rip her jeans off, shove his face in her sweet little cunt, and eat her for breakfast. He'd give her whatever she wanted, however she wanted it, for as long as she could take it. Then it was going to be his turn. And he planned to take a long, hard, sweaty time.

"Do you, um, want some coffee?" she finally asked, interrupting his ill-timed fantasy. Her eyes focused on his chin, his chest, anywhere but his telling green stare. Now that they were completely alone, she wasn't quite able to meet the lust-driven fire smoldering there. "Or some breakfast?"

Hell yeah, he thought with a hungry groan. I'd like to open your soaked pussy with my thumbs and taste you from your clit to your slit, licking my way as deep into you as I can.

Whoa. What was it with him and this sudden oral fixation? Hell, he liked going down on a woman as well as the next guy—but he'd never felt this burning, gut-clawing ache for the taste of a woman's cunt in his entire life, like he'd go nuts without it. He felt himself actually tremble, barely managing to mumble, "Yeah, some coffee would be great."

"Okay, great," she repeated too brightly, obviously relieved to have something to do.

It was easy to see he was making her nervous as hell. Not that he blamed her. He'd meant to be subtle, to ease into this, but one look at her and he was tumbling hard and fast, unable to put on the friggin' brakes. He should've known that after all this time he wouldn't be able to play it cool around her. It was all he could do to keep his ass in his chair and not drop to his knees on the hardwood boards, begging like a fool.

But he'd do it if he had to. No one who'd ever known him would've ever believed it. He knew he had a badass, ruthless reputation, not to mention a notoriously wicked one with women. But he'd do whatever it took to make Taylor Moore his own.

Beg.

Plead.

Anything.

She moved about the airy kitchen with the smooth grace that had dazzled him as a boy and seduced him as a man. She was just so perfectly delicate and precise; it made a guy ache to watch her go all flushed and ripe, begging for him to shove his cock into her and ride her as hard as he dared. He watched the elegant lines of her body in profile as she leaned up to pull down two thick, terracotta colored mugs, and her shirt rose just high enough to give him a brief glimpse of the pale skin between its hem and her jeans.

Well, hell. His cock was on the verge of bursting open and he hadn't even seen anything more than a smooth inch of skin yet.

But it was Taylor's naked flesh he was seeing, and that right there made all the difference. "This was a mistake," he groaned into the heavy silence. "We can't do this here."

She gave him an uneasy look. "Do what?"

"Talk," he grumbled, watching the way the early morning rays of sunlight glinted through the windows, setting the red highlights in her long dark hair on fire. "All I keep thinking about is how we're alone and how much I want to be inside of you. But you're not ready yet. We need to get all this shit out in the open first, before we make love."

She wasn't ready? Make love?

Man, she really needed more sleep if she was going to be able to keep up with his lightning-speed pace. Why had she stayed up half the night painting? She should've been saving her strength! Was it not even thirty minutes since Jake had walked up behind her in Mason's and started turning her entire world upside down?

She took a deep breath and turned to face him, clutching the counter behind her for support. Jake's eyes moved over her from the top of her head down to her toes, making her tingle everywhere in between. Geez, this man was potent. Her skin was feeling tight, as if it were suddenly too small for her body, while her blood seemed to have trouble keeping up with the furious pounding of her heart.

"Taylor," he rasped, staring straight at the delicate slopes of her breasts, "you are so fucking beautiful. You blow my mind."

A startled, shocked burst of laughter escaped her. "You must be blind, Jake. I'm, uh, just me."

"Yeah, I know." He nodded his head in agreement. "Just you. The sexiest thing I've ever laid eyes on. Do you know you haven't changed at all?"

His eyes moved over every inch of her, then did a slow, detailed exploration of her face and the soft tendrils of hair that framed it. "You look just the same. I know it sounds trite as hell, but it's like you've been waiting for me all this time."

I have, she thought with desperation, wishing she had the nerve to just come right out and say it. But he was like a big, dangerous animal, and she knew better than to get too close. Still, she wasn't sure it was him she didn't trust — or her.

Yeah, right. Please. She knew she trusted Jake. She was the one with the control problem here, at least around him.

He stood up, but made no move to leave. Taylor kept her eyes on his, afraid of what she might do if she got caught staring at the huge bulge of his crotch again. She had horrified visions of herself begging him to take it out and let her play.

Jake shoved his hands flat in his back pockets, blew out a tense breath, and nodded to the painting hanging over her right shoulder. "When did you do that one?"

Her eyes dropped despite her good intentions and she gulped. Oh, man. Did he even realize what he was doing to her? She struggled to drag her gaze away from the sinful sight of his jeans stretched tight across his groin, the beautiful bulge indecently accentuated by his casual pose, and tried to focus on the painting instead. It was one of her favorites; a depiction of a Faerie Lord kneeling by a lily covered pool, his back to the viewer, while Wood Nymphs lured him into the crystal water. For one horrified moment she thought Jake might've recognized the image was actually his own, but the face was thankfully turned away.

She looked back at Jake to find him watching her, a strange expression of hunger and tenderness burning in his eyes. "How do you know I did this?" Her voice held a subtle note of suspicion. "Maybe I bought it somewhere."

He smiled at her, and she couldn't help but notice that his smile looked just a tad guilty. Her eyes narrowed, but Jake only laughed and said, "Just because I barely talked to you doesn't mean I didn't watch you like a hawk. You always had a sketchbook under your arm and paint on your fingers."

Her lips twitched. "Are you by any chance calling me an art geek?"

Jake held up his hands in surrender. "Art goddess, honey." His smile widened. "Definitely a goddess."

She shook her head at his outrageousness. "I still could've bought this painting from another artist. I might not even paint anymore."

Jake snorted, taking a long look around the beautiful kitchen. "Living in a place like this? I'm not buying it. No way in hell could you afford this on Mitch's sheriff's salary. I'd say you're not only still painting, sweetheart, but that you're making a shit load of money at it."

"Maybe I'm a scorching day trader," she countered, but her eyes were shining with laughter.

He took a step closer, and then another. "Yeah, and maybe I'm a ballerina."

Her brows lifted in mock surprise. "You don't think I look like a scorching day trader, Jake?"

His eyes did another blazing inspection of her body, ending on her lush, petal soft lips. "I think you look like you could be anything you wanted to be, Taylor."

And fuckable. You look very, very fuckable. "But I already know you painted it, 'cause I recognize your style."

Uh-oh. "Yeah? Did you used to sneak peeks at my sketchbook when I wasn't looking?"

"Naw, I just used to snake the ones you'd given to Mitch outta his room. Used to piss the hell out of him."

"I always wondered what happened to all those sketches," she admitted in a quiet voice, her eyes softening to a warm, liquid brown. "Mitch said he lost them or they'd gotten thrown away."

Jake moved forward, only a few remaining feet separating them. "I still have them, Taylor," he admitted with that small, crooked smile of his. "I even had them framed and hung them all over my house."

Oh, Jesus, she didn't know what to say. All that would come out was a soft, breathless, "Jake," and they could both hear the heartache and need in his name.

He rubbed his hands together, then shoved them back in his pockets, the front ones this time, before he did something stupid and grabbed her again. "Hell, I'm going to go now, while I still can. I'll be back at six to pick you up and we'll grab dinner somewhere." His breath expelled on a harsh sigh. "Some place nice and crowded so I know I won't be able to grope you. That way maybe we'll be able to get everything said first."

"And then what?" The minute the words left her mouth, she wanted to die. She sounded far too anxious about what they were going to be doing after they ate dinner together. And Jake was studying her with the hungry anticipation of a man looking forward to a juicy steak after years of nothing but bread and water. Should she warn him she was more of the saltines variety, bland and dry and uninspiring?

But then again, just looking at him made her feel wet and needy and deliciously warm.

His killer smile flashed this time, the same one that had made all the girls chase after him when they were younger. It was just as potent. Still just as dangerous to her equilibrium.

"Then I get to grope you." Yeah, then I get to cram you full of my cock and we can spend the rest of our lives fucking like minks.

Taylor smiled despite herself. "You always did have a way with words, Jake Farrell."

Oh babe, he thought. *If you only knew.*

"Gimme a break here, all right," he teased, shaking his head at his own inability to be smooth around the one woman he'd always wanted to smooth-talk. "It's hard to be witty and cool when all your blood's rushing outta one head and into the other."

She couldn't stop the laugh this time. When was the last time she'd felt like this? Had she ever felt like this? No, nothing in life had ever come close to being near this man. Not even winning the prestigious Caldecott Medal, her most prized moment, the only thing in her life until now that had given it substance and validation. But Jake could give it meaning, if he'd let her love him. It was a foolish thought, but one she couldn't help entertaining. A girl had to have her dreams or she just shriveled up and died, didn't she? And her dream had always been Jake.

Maybe it was time to just dive in and grab hold of him. If she didn't, wasn't she going to hate herself for the rest of her life, knowing she'd just let him walk away from her a second time? Hadn't she always known, deep down inside in that sweet place of dreams and longing and intuition that he was going to walk back into her life one day, claiming what was his? And it was her. She was his. She always had been. It was just Mitch who had always stood between them, and now he was gone.

"Do you like Italian?" she heard herself ask. It was amazing she was able to sound so calm when her heart was racing, pounding with need and anticipation. "Angelo opened a restaurant over in Pressmore, off of Chester. It's lovely if you'd like to go there."

"Angie? I can't believe he's hung around here all these years."

"He married Sandy Fuller and they've stayed here ever since. They have five kids and she's pregnant with their sixth."

Jake shook his head in amused horror, thinking of the hulking tight end who used to swear he'd never settle down. "Damn, that bastard's been busy."

The corner of Taylor's mouth lifted. "Yeah, well, so has Sandy."

And just like that they fell into another one of those weird silences, just staring at each other like they wanted to eat the other person alive. The sexual tension arcing between them could've powered the whole blasted town it was so electric. It was a giving, living force that moved from one to the other, gaining intensity with each rebound. A charged, pulsing glow that she could feel raising the baby fine hairs along her body. She was even sweating despite the early morning chill still in the air.

She broke before he did, cringing when she heard herself suddenly ask, "What are you going to do today?"

Holy cow! Where in the hell did that come from? It was so strange, this possessive little bug creeping beneath her skin that didn't want to let him out of her sight. She'd never felt it before, not even with Mitch. He'd always been more of everyone else's before he'd ever been hers, not that she'd ever really wanted him. But Jake had been gone for over a year when Mitch proposed, and her domineering mother had pushed her to settle for what she could get. God, she'd been so incredibly stupid. So miserably stupid and young and naïve.

If she'd ever asked Mitch what his plans were, he'd have told her to mind her own business. Jake just smiled though, as if he could see straight through her and knew she wanted him to stay with her. As if he wanted the same thing, or really wanted to drag her along with him. He looked so cocky and self-assured and arrogantly pleased by such a stupid little question.

"I'm going to drive out to Pressmore and check into the Hilton they have over there, then drop by my uncle's place. I haven't talked to him since he tracked me down two days ago to tell me he'd heard you and Mitch were divorced. Then I'm going to pace my hotel room waiting till it's time to come pick you up."

"Oh."

Oh? What was it with her and these stupid comebacks? The man was going to think she was an idiot if she didn't start stringing more words together. Problem was, it was hard to get your tongue to work right when it kept wanting to hang out of your mouth and pant like a dog. She wanted him so bad she could practically taste it.

Who was she kidding? She wanted to taste it — every single beautiful, muscled inch of him!

And what was he talking about? Why had his uncle had to track him down? Why had he thought Jake would even care she was divorced in the first place? And what in the hell was she supposed to do now?

"I mean —" She broke off, shifting from foot to foot, her whole body itching with need. She wanted to rub up against him like a cat, stroking her body against his own, skin to skin, and scratch this itch once and for all.

Mmm. Wow. Jake Farrell as a boy had been her ideal, but looking at him all grown up was almost too good to be true. "What I mean is — why don't we talk now?" she asked, knowing her voice was getting huskier by the second. "I trust you to be able to control yourself."

"That makes one of us," Jake muttered, his eyes dropping to her chest again, fascinated by the sight of her nipples poking against the starched white cotton of her shirt. How in the fuck was he supposed to control himself when he knew she wanted him, was getting aroused, was probably already nice and wet? Shit, he couldn't do it. He had to get the hell outta there.

"No. I'm not going to rush you right into this," he gritted through his clenched teeth, barely holding himself together. "We're going to do it right, damn it, because after tonight, there's no going back, Taylor. I've waited too long for this. I want you to be right there with me, with everything out in the open. No secrets, no lies. Just you and me and everything else that's going to come later on."

Like marriage and family and staying together till we die, he thought. Hell, even death wasn't going to keep him away from this woman. He needed to give her this last day to come to grips with what he'd just landed at her dainty feet. But that was all the fair warning he was willing to give.

She nodded in fascinated agreement, clearly not knowing what to make of him. Probably not believing a word he said.

"And for God's sake, don't wear anything too sexy or I'll lose it and all my good intentions will fly right out the fucking window."

"I, um, think you'll be safe." She tucked a glossy strand of hair behind her ear and sent him a wry smile. "I seriously doubt I own anything a man like you would find sexy."

Jake ground his jaw, unleashing a frustrated groan. "Hell, you don't have a clue, babe." His eyes flicked over her casual clothes, lingering on all the sweet spots. "You're not even showing me any skin and I'm already aching. Just try to have mercy on me, okay?"

Big brown eyes blinked in awe. "Uh, okay."

He looked like he wanted to kiss her again, but forced himself to the door instead. Once there, he turned back, treating her to another long, lingering, hungry look. "And Taylor," he growled, unable to tear his eyes from her denim covered crotch.

"Yes?"

"Pack a bag, honey. We'll come back for everything else later."

Chapter 4

Taylor's heart nearly jumped out of her throat when the first knock sounded. Yikes! It was only a quarter to! The blasted man was fifteen minutes early on the most important night of her life. How could he? It was unforgivable, she thought desperately, running around her bedroom wearing nothing but her brand new, midnight-blue lace bra and panties set and a light brushing of make-up. She wanted—no, needed—to look her absolute best and here she was not even dressed yet!

Running to the window—the one that looked out over the bougainvillea covered, latticed arch of her front doorway—Taylor looked down through the diamond openings and violet blooms to see him raising his fist for another round of shake-the-walls-down knocking. He looked too sexy to be real, wearing soft, faded khakis, a hunter green polo, and brown work boots. Oh, God. She wanted to wring his neck for being early and throw herself all over him for looking so delicious all at the same time.

His fist lifted to knock again, and she could see from the set of his broad shoulders that he was starting to get worried. Did he think she'd run off? Stood him up? Hah! She may feel sick to her stomach with excitement, but she wasn't a moron. If Jake Farrell wanted to use her for a night, or a fling, or whatever the hell he wanted, she wasn't going to argue. She didn't for one moment believe he wanted anything emotional from her, but she was willing to take what she could get and wring it of pleasure.

Actually, she was going to grab hold with both hands and hang on for as long as she could, then live with the heart-stopping memories for the rest of her life.

She'd cherish them.

Savor them.

Survive on them.

The next round of vigorous knocking jolted her out of her lovesick stupor. She quickly wrapped her champagne satin robe around her and threw open the window. "Jake, I'm here," she called down, feeling like an idiot for letting him knock for so long. Where in God's name had her mind been? On Jake, that's where. She clutched the robe tight across her chest as he stepped back off the porch, far enough to see her over the flower-covered arch. "I'm, um, sorry, but I'm not ready yet." Then, with a pointed stare, she muttered, "You're early."

Jake's eyes moved over her like a brush on canvas. They stroked her skin, painting her with beauty—making her feel like a sexy, desirable woman for the first time in her life. She flushed again, wondering if she was always going to look sunburned around the man. Thank God she'd gone easy on the blusher or she might start looking like Wanda, and then she'd have to kill herself. There wouldn't be any other option.

Jake just kept staring—and staring. "Damn, Taylor," he groaned, eyeing the clasp of her hands at the front edges of her robe. His lips parted, cheekbones tinged with a deep flush of arousal. "Are you naked under that little thing?"

"No," she laughed, feeling like she'd been caught in some modern rendition of a Shakespearian balcony scene. Move over Juliet, here comes Taylor Moore. "I left the door unlocked, so you can come on in. I'll be down in just a sec."

Jake eyed the ivy-covered trellis leading up to her window. "I could always climb up and lend you a hand."

Her knuckles gripped the champagne satin tighter. "Uh, that won't be necessary, but, um, thanks anyway."

His sensual lips lifted in an unmistakably wicked grin. "You don't have to be shy with me, Taylor. What difference will it make if I see you putting it on, honey, when I'm gonna be the one takin' it off you later anyway?"

She shook her head at his outrageousness, stunned by the girlish giggle bubbling up out of her. She was utterly unaware of the provocative picture she made smiling down at him from the backlit room, her body a shadowy, sensual silhouette in the soft light of the window. "And if I had a dollar for every time you've probably said those words to a woman, Jake Farrell, I'd be richer than Bill Gates."

His smile fell. "No, you wouldn't."

The twinkle in her eye said she wasn't buying it. Not for a second. "There's no reason to be coy, you know. I remember your reputation. That much couldn't have changed in the last ten years."

"Then you should also remember that I never had to work very hard at getting a girl." His dark green eyes burned with lust, making her breath pant in little bursts of need. "Too bad the only one I ever wanted was you. And that sure as hell hasn't changed."

Maybe she felt safe because of the distance between them, or maybe she was just finally grown up enough to swallow her insecurities and go after what she wanted. Whatever the reason, Taylor tried for a provocative smile and said, "But this time you're going to get me, aren't you?"

Uh-oh. His entire body went rigid at her words, big hands fisting at his sides, and she felt the nerves she'd swallowed down quickly working their way right back up. Her eyes must have shown her panic, because he suddenly growled, "Don't even think about it."

Taylor licked her lips. "Think about what?"

"Taking it back. You said it, now you're going to have to back it up."

Her spine went straight, shoulders back, eyes narrowed. "Maybe I'm ready to back it up." Hah! So there!

She was feeling pretty proud of herself till he grunted, "Then hold that thought," and promptly disappeared through her front door. Well hell, now what? Her eyes flew across her room in a near state of panic, wondering what to do. Geez, why hadn't she kept her big mouth shut? She really did have every intention of going through with this thing and throwing herself all over the gorgeous man tonight, but she'd been planning on working up to it over dinner. Not to mention having a few heady glasses of wine to help her along.

Her frantic gaze finally landed on her bed, where she'd laid out her new outfit for tonight. Yes! But she was too late. She made a mad grab for the clothes just as Jake appeared in her doorway, and he just kept right on coming, not stopping until he was standing over her.

God, the man was tall. She bent back her head and looked up, higher and higher, finding herself trapped by his brilliant green eyes. They—burned on her. There was no other word for it. "What are you doing?" she squeaked, wincing at the ridiculous sound.

He took a step closer.

She took a quick step back and felt the bed hit the backs of her knees. He wasn't even touching her yet, just staring down at her, but his look told her exactly what he was thinking about, down to the last slippery, delicious detail. She flushed and felt herself go hot and wet between her trembling legs, her pussy eagerly readying itself for him. His nostrils flared the tiniest bit, and she moaned at the thought that he might actually be able to smell the need on her.

Jake took another deep breath and nearly died. She smelled so damn good. Good enough to eat. To lick. To tongue fuck for hours on end. His voice emerged as little more than a husky growl. "Your cunt's already getting wet for me, isn't it, Taylor?"

She groaned this time, her eyes snapping shut, as if she could block him out simply by taking away the incredible sight of him. It didn't work. She could still smell his own delicious scent; still feel the waves of heat and lust coming off of him, crashing against her. "Jake, I have to get ready." Her voice felt thick, everything within her going heavy with want.

His big hands covered her small ones where they still clasped the front of her robe together. "Like I said, I'll help you, sweetheart."

His voice seemed to shake as much as her fingers and he felt a violent rush of love flow through him, sharp and indescribably sweet. He couldn't believe he was here. He'd wanted her for so long, and here he was, standing in her bedroom with her, while she trembled before him, barely dressed and smelling sweetly of desire. This was it. The best moment of his life. Right here, right now. And he could hardly wait for all the ones just like it to come.

She cracked her lids enough to catch a peek of him through the thick fringe of her lashes. Oh, man. The way he looked at her, as if she were the most desirable woman in all the world, made her want to run to her mirror and look to check if she was still the same ol' Taylor. Maybe some childhood wish had been granted and she'd finally grown boobs and hips. Maybe hell had frozen over and she'd been transformed into a Victoria's Secret model without even realizing it.

She did a quick mental inventory, but everything still felt the same. Well, hell. What was wrong with this guy? He could have any woman he wanted, and yet, here he was with her, looking as if he wanted to eat her alive. Was there something she'd never seen, maybe? Some hidden allure that she'd never recognized? Or was he just crazy? Blind as a bat?

Then he smiled, and her eyes narrowed with suspicion. That was more like it. Taylor could easily imagine him finding her less-than-perfect curves—okay, pretty much nonexistent curves something to laugh at. "What's so funny?"

"Nothing's funny, babe. I'm just happy. I've never had to coax a woman out of her clothes before, and it's a hell of a lot more fun than I've ever thought it'd be." His green eyes crinkled at the corners, looking sexy as sin. "Then again, I think it's just the idea of getting you outta your clothes that makes it fun."

Taylor groaned. "Jake, why do you keep saying these things?"

"Because they're true, honey," he replied in the kind of tone a parent might use on a reluctant child. "And after tonight, you're not ever going to have any trouble believing me again. Now let go and let me see what you're hiding under there."

She laughed softly; a sound more pain than humor. "Nothing, Jake. That's the problem. I'm not hiding anything. What you see is what you get."

"Good, because it's exactly what I want." His hands tightened on hers, forcing them away. "Stop teasing me, Taylor. Let me see you."

He sounded so sincere, so tortured; she couldn't help but look up at him in wonder. And she just kept watching him as she felt the satin soft fabric part and the cool air of the early evening hit her skin. But she wasn't cold. There was enough heat in Jake's stare to make her sweat. His work-rough hands moved to her shoulders, pushing the robe away until it fell to the floor in a silent swoosh of fabric. Then his fingers tightened, biting into the smooth slope of her shoulder, almost hard enough to make her wince.

"Aw, damn," he whispered into the heavy, breath filled silence. "Do you have any idea how beautiful you are?"

This time it was a moan that escaped her. "Jake, you really are blind."

Though his hands stayed on her shoulders, his eyes touched her everywhere. He couldn't get enough of her perfect, upturned breasts. They were small, yes, but couldn't she see how sexy they were, their tiny nipples tilted up, just begging to be sucked and licked and scraped with his teeth? "I love the bra, babe, but I'd rather see what's underneath it."

His eyes locked with hers, filled with an eagerness she couldn't help but respond to. He looked like a little boy on

Christmas morning getting ready to unwrap his favorite present.

"Can I take it off you?"

She was surprised he even asked, but then, his look told her this would be the only time. Once she gave him permission, she was going to be his to do with as he pleased, however and whenever he wanted. She licked her lips again and gave a slight nod of her head.

Before her next breath, the front clasp between the pert mounds was released and Jake's warm, rough palms were molding over her naked flesh. He squeezed, then slowly rotated his hands so that her swollen nipples chafed against his calloused skin. Oh, God help her. That felt so good. A strange, jungle cat sound purred in the back of her throat, shocking them both. Jake's hands tightened, and she felt the shudder that shot straight through him.

"You like that, don't you, sweetheart?"

Something like a sob, or maybe a wail, whimpered from her throat. She couldn't decide if she wanted to sink to the floor in embarrassment or grab his hands and hold them to her tighter. Then he leaned down, nuzzling the side of her neck, and asked, "Do you want more?"

"Yes, please."

She felt his smile against her skin, his warm breath sending a shiver through her increasingly heavy limbs. It was almost like floating, this feeling, and yet she was anchored in place, unwilling to move and miss so much as a second of it. His hands shifted so that his palms cupped the tender undersides, testing their weight. "Mmm," she moaned, thinking that felt heavenly. Then his thumbs flicked over her rigid nipples and a sharp cry burst from her throat. "Oh, God."

"I agree," he groaned, grasping the hard, pink tips and twisting with his fingertips, using just enough pressure to make her gasp. He opened his mouth against the side of her neck and flicked his tongue against her dewy skin, growling from the taste of her. Damn, he wanted to do so many fucking things—everything to this woman, but he already felt on the verge of losing it and all he'd done was touch her beautiful, precious breasts.

For a split second, Jake considered shoving her back on the bed and starting their marathon night of fucking right now, this very second. God only knew his cock was ready, pounding against the fly of his pants the way it was, begging to be let out to play, but his heart knew this needed to be done right. He'd promised her dinner and answers, and he was going to give them to her even if it killed him to have to wait. And it just might.

Obviously, the first priority was to get her covered up again, or they'd never even make it out of the room. What had he been thinking, torturing himself with this little peek at paradise? Huh! He'd been thinking with the wrong head, that's what, and now he was just going to have to force himself to stop copping the best damn feel of his life and cover the woman back up. A turtleneck would've been handy, considering his maddening state of lust, but he made do with what was available. Cursing beneath his breath, Jake fumbled with the clasp of her bra. As soon as it clicked back into place, he grabbed blindly at the clothes he'd seen lying on the bed behind her.

"Here," he grunted, pulling back from her enough to look at what he held in his hands. "We need to get you dressed or I'm gonna be crammed deep before you even know what hit you."

Sensing the urgency in his words, Taylor grabbed at her top and quickly pulled it over her head, while Jake struggled to keep his eyes away from the smooth expanse of her pale belly and the delectable little patch of lace barely concealing the dark curls between her legs. He tried, but failed miserably, leaning back to get a clearer view of the neat little triangle barely visible through the blue lace. His nostrils flared. He could smell the warm, subtle scent of her cunt, like cinnamon and vanilla, and any second now his face was going to be shoved right there, his tongue searching for her flavor, but then she bent over to pull on her skirt.

All he could think about was pulling it right back off of her.

When she straightened again, completely dressed but for her narrow feet, he cursed some more beneath his breath, then not so beneath his breath as he muttered, "What the fuck is that?"

Taylor noted his narrowed glare, wondering what the problem was. "This? It's just something I picked up for tonight. I drove over to the mall today and bought it."

He looked—stunned. Pained, even. Taylor looked down at herself, but couldn't figure it out. The dark blue matching silk skirt and tank looked just as it had when she'd tried it on earlier at the department store. She couldn't figure out what the problem was. It was maybe a bit more revealing than she felt comfortable with, but certainly nothing that should've shocked Jake. "What's wrong with it?"

He grunted at her. Actually grunted. "Jesus, Taylor. I told you not to wear anything sexy and you go and buy this!"

She didn't care for his tone. The outfit wasn't that revealing, for crying out loud. "What's wrong with this?"

Jake sent her a pained look. "I don't even know where to start." His hand motioned toward to her chest, and he muttered, "The fabric's so soft that I can clearly see the outline of your nipples." His eyes dropped to the thin strip of flesh visible between the hem of her top and the waist of her full-length poet's skirt. "And I can see your belly," he added in a grumble. "And that damn skirt's so sexy—I just want to toss it over your head and fuck you senseless while you're still wearing it!"

She couldn't help it; she smiled.

"You think this is funny?" he gritted through his teeth, reaching out for her hand and pressing it over the enormous mass of his cock straining against the front of his pants. She sucked her breath in sharply, but didn't try to pull her hand away, curling her fingers around him instead. "I don't know how funny you're going to find it when I have to walk through the restaurant with a fucking boner trying to bust through my pants?"

A startled laugh escaped her, but Jake only groaned in answer, pushing her hand away. Then he grabbed hold of it and dragged her along with him. He needed to get the hell away from her bed and quickly or he really was going to lose it. They'd already made it to the top of the stairs before she managed to stop laughing and say, "Jake, wait, I need my shoes."

He stopped, squeezed his eyes shut, and counted to ten. Without looking back at her, he mumbled, "You go back and grab 'em and I'll wait for you out front."

Her fingers slipped from his, and he asked, "Where's your bags?"

Here it was, do or die time. "I, ah, left them in the kitchen."

The breath he hadn't even realized he'd been holding released in a burst of intense relief. He forced himself down the stairs, struggling to keep his body from turning around and following her right back into that room, locking the door, and keeping her in bed for the next sixty or so years, trapped beneath his body and his cock.

Food first, man. Food, then the fucking, and then forever.

Chapter 5

"So, Jake Farrell, what have you done with your life?"

He smiled and leaned back to get as comfortable as a man his size could get in such a small chair. The restaurant was perfect, their cozy private corner ideal for the conversation he had in mind. The ride over had been quick and quiet, thick with sexual tension, but the soothing ambience of Angelo's was slowly helping Taylor to relax. And the table was small enough to have her easily within his reach. Considering all that, Jake would've been happy sitting on a crate. "Where would you like me to start?"

She took a small sip of wine to cover her nerves. Of course, it would've helped if her hand weren't shaking so badly. "Start at the beginning, from the moment you left."

From the moment you left me.

His jaw tightened, his eyes eating hers. "I didn't want to go." His tone was low, but forceful with the honesty of his words.

She gave a small smile, unaware of the sadness — the loneliness that shone through. "But you did. Where to?"

He studied her for a moment, and then he said, "You know my parents died when I was ten." He didn't wait for an answer, but just kept talking. "I lived here with my father's brother, my Uncle Mark. I have another uncle, this one my mother's little brother, who lives in upstate Washington. His name's Frank. Anyway, I drove my old pickup outta town and went to live with him, worked my way through college, and then started my own business with a loan from both of them." He smiled. "Which I paid back within two years."

He'd given her only the bones of his existence, leaving out the lonely years of longing. For her. It was going to take time to convince her, he knew—but there was no denying the impatience to make her understand now.

She laughed softly. "Jake Farrell's life in thirty seconds, huh? Somehow," she drawled, clucking her tongue, "I think there's a lot you're not telling me."

One dark brow rose. "Yeah?"

"Uh-huh. For instance, what kind of business do you own?"

"I'm a contractor."

"Really? What do you contract?"

Jake laughed, loving everything about her. "Houses, honey." He held out his calloused palms. "I build houses."

"Ooh!" She looked so excited, scooting closer in her chair. "That's so wonderful. I mean—how fascinating. God, I bet you're wonderful at it."

Her faith in him was staggering. With his head cocked to the side, his eyes trying to read her, he said, "Why would you say that?"

"A fellow artist's instincts," she replied with a warm smile, completely at ease for the moment. "They zing every time I look at you, Jake."

His eyes flared with heat and she suddenly realized what she'd just said. Oh, God, she groaned. Her instincts zinging? She might as well come right out and tell the blasted man she was completely fascinated with him— obsessed with him—head over heels in love with him! She needed to change the subject. Quick! "Where do you live?" she asked too brightly, wincing at the desperate sound of her voice.

Jake took pity on her for the moment, but he wasn't going to let her avoid the subject forever. "I'm still living in Washington, but I might be moving soon."

Her eyes went wide. "Really? Where?"

Wherever you decide you want me to build our house.

He waited while their waiter brought out fresh, mouthwatering breadsticks and their salads, refilled their glasses, and then murmured, "It hasn't been decided yet." She gave him a questioning look, but he didn't offer to elaborate. "And what about you?" he asked around a bite of crisp romaine and croutons.

She smiled. "You already know where I live and that I paint."

And that's all you're going to know.

No way in hell was she going to tell him about her books. Oh, she'd have loved to be able to share her success, but the truth he'd see on those pages would be too humiliating to endure.

Jake took a long swallow of wine, waiting for her to open up even though he knew she wasn't going to. This was going to be the hardest wall to scale, but the most rewarding in the end. And God, he was scared to death of her reaction. If she panicked and ran out on him, he didn't know what in the hell he'd do. Chase after her, of course, but then what? How do you convince a woman that you love her more than anything in the world? How do you make her understand that you can't live another day without her? He had a good idea how to prove his point physically, but would it be enough emotionally?

They dropped the topic for the moment, making casual talk about the restaurant and Sandy and Angelo's success while they dug into the food. But as soon as their plates were cleared and their entrees served, Jake cut right to the heart of what he wanted to know. "So," he murmured, scooping up a forkful of steaming lasagna, "why'd you marry him?"

Taylor laughed, but not because the question was funny. No, she laughed at herself. Why had she married Mitch? Lord if she knew. Yeah, her sorry excuse for a mother had pushed her into it, wanting her hands cleared of a daughter so she could hit the road, but there had to have been more to it than that. Maybe she'd done it out of fear, or anger, or hell — she really didn't know why she'd done it. Instead of answering, she asked, "Why'd you leave?"

His jaw hardened as he swallowed. He didn't want to think about the night before he'd driven out of town. Didn't want to remember all his mistakes and the things he should've done — should've said. But Taylor deserved answers.

She deserved everything.

"Because I couldn't take the fact that you were with him. Couldn't stand hearing about the two of you together one more day. I was going crazy with it. Hell, I didn't trust myself not to do something stupid and kill the asshole."

Her expression was guarded, as if she didn't know quite what to make of his words. "I always thought Mitch was your friend?"

Jake fell back against his chair, looking out at the endless night through the open window. His eyes clouded with regret, as if he were seeing the past and all its mistakes play out before him. "I don't even really know how to explain it, Taylor. Mitch was more like family. We grew up together. Spent our lives together. His mom babied me like I was her own. Nothing had ever come between us till you. I didn't know how to handle it and the bastard knew it. He saw the way I looked at you when I thought nobody was watching, and so he rubbed it in my face every chance he got, the fact he had you and I didn't."

"But he didn't have me, Jake." Her voice was quiet, soft, while she pushed her Chicken Marsala around with her fork. "Not until after you'd gone, anyway."

Jake's eyes snapped back to hers, demanding an answer. "Why'd you marry him, Taylor? You knew what he was like." His tone was more curious than accusing.

Was there really an answer here? One that even remotely made sense? Her hands clenched her napkin beneath the table, twisting as if she might wring the truth from the wrinkled linen. "Maybe it was just because you were gone. You left without saying goodbye, Jake. It was stupid and childish, I know. I mean you hated me, right? Why should I have cared that you were gone?"

She shrugged, looking suddenly embarrassed and unsure, not quite able to meet his eyes anymore. "But it was like something died inside of me and I just didn't care anymore. I think I'd gone out with him all that time just to be closer to you. Not that that made any sense either, because you always ignored me. You never even really talked to me, and I had no reason to think Mitch might've lied about you not liking me."

His hand caught hers under the table, holding it tight enough to hurt her fingers. She didn't think he even realized how he held her, as if he were afraid she'd slip away from him again. "If I'd thought for one fucking moment that you wanted me, I'd have taken you with me, Taylor. I've been waiting my whole life to—"

He broke off at her stunned expression. She was going all shocked and flushed on him again because he was running away with himself, losing control. He took a long, slow breath, struggling for calm.

Sanity.

Patience.

"Okay," he finally said, "let's hold that thought and try another route. I know Mitch didn't keep his hands off your sweet little ass, so how in the hell did you keep from getting pregnant?" He knew Mitch would've wanted a child, seeing a baby as a way of holding Taylor to him forever.

She blushed clear to her roots, looking sunburned. "I went on the pill, but even then I still made him wear a— you know."

"You made him wear a rubber?" Jake snorted, his eyes wide with stunned surprise. He'd have thought it was funny as hell, if he could've found anything funny in the thought of the two of them together. But he couldn't, because it made him sick and angry and thirsty for the bastard's blood to think of Mitch's hands on Taylor. All the times he'd had the privilege of sleeping beside her body. The times when he'd sunk inside of her and become a part of her.

Mitch must've been the biggest fool alive to have destroyed his chance with Taylor Moore. He was a pig through and through—which meant that he and ol' Wanda Merton were perfect for each other.

Taylor's shoulders stiffened at his tone. "Of course I made him wear protection. Every single time," she said tightly, "not that there were all that many times to worry about. I may have been naïve, but I wasn't that stupid. I knew he'd slept around, that he still did, that he always would. I wasn't willing to take any chances. And after awhile, he got tired of it anyway."

Jake snorted again. "Yeah, right. More like his miserable little dick couldn't take the fact that he couldn't make you come." His eyes pinned her, demanding she hold his stare. "And he couldn't, could he?"

Her slim shoulders hunched, as if she were trying to close in on herself. "It really wasn't his fault, Jake. It's me. Something's just wrong with me or—oh, I don't know. I can't really explain it. I don't even really like sex, if you want to know the truth. I'm awkward and it hurts and I just don't get what the big deal is. Not unless—" she snapped her mouth shut, unwilling to give him the entire truth, which was that she only got excited when thinking about having sex with him.

Jake sat straight up in his chair, the tiny table separating them so insubstantial it was almost forgotten. "He hurt you?" he demanded, his tone violent and angry.

It took her a moment to understand what he meant. "Not on purpose. I really think it was just me."

The last thing in the world he ever wanted to think about was Taylor letting Mitch slide between her slender, silky thighs, but he couldn't stop himself from pressing her for all the dirty little details. He was like a madman; he had to know it all. "I'm not buying it," he grumbled, his jaw working as if he had to force the bitter words out. "You're telling me that screwing was just painful for you with him? Was he too big, or did you really have trouble getting wet with him?"

And was he really going to be able to keep down his lasagna listening to this?

"I don't know." She clearly hated the topic, looking both frustrated and uncomfortable, and as if she was seriously beginning to consider wringing his neck. "I didn't get very wet — there, so maybe he was just, um, too big."

Not good, Jake thought with a groan. Hell, he'd grown up with Mitch. He knew the size of the guy's cock, and it wasn't anything to brag about. Not small, but average, and he was anything but. Shit, if sex with Mitch hurt, she was probably gonna run screaming when she saw the size of his own hard-on. He was about twice as thick as Mitch and had a good three and a half inches on him in length. Of course, the fact that she hadn't been wet enough would've made it more painful for her. Mitch wasn't only a total prick, but a lousy-ass lover as well. It was all Jake could do to bite back a satisfied smile.

He cleared his throat, took a long sip of his wine, and tried again. "All right. Let's talk about why you weren't wet."

She groaned long and low, slinking down further in her chair. "Do we have to? It's bad enough even telling you this stuff, Jake. Why do we have go into detail?"

Because I'm a sick bastard who can't get off enough on knowing that your sex life was hell, he thought with a vicious curse. To Taylor, he simply said, "Because I just have to know, all right?"

She shrugged in response, trying to pull her hand loose from his, but he wasn't letting go. Instead, he grabbed the other one, holding both beneath the table, hidden from view by the white and red checked tablecloth.

His thumbs drew small, lazy circles into her soft palms as he scooted his chair closer. He didn't stop until his knees practically bracketed her hips and he could reach what he wanted. Then he let go of her hands and placed his rough palms on the tops of her slender thighs.

She jumped and grabbed at his thick wrists, but was no match for his strength. She couldn't even wrap her hands around them, much less budge him.

"What are you doing?" she asked in a horrified whisper, her eyes darting around to make sure no one was paying them any attention.

"Relax, Taylor." He kneaded the firm muscles beneath his palms, edging higher and higher until his fingertips grazed the crease of her hip and pubic bone. She went absolutely stock-still—wasn't even breathing. "Take a deep breath and tell me why you didn't get wet when he fucked you."

She wasn't having any trouble getting wet right now. "Because he wasn't you," she blurted before she was able to stop the words. He was frying her brain and she was making a complete fool of herself. Why did these things keep flying out of her mouth? "I mean, uh—"

"No, your first answer was just fine, babe." His hands tightened and his own breathing became deeper. Slow and deep and heavy. "Did he try to get you hot? Did he always play with your cunt before he fucked you? Did he finger you first?"

Loud flaming fire engine red. God, she blushed so bright it practically blinded him.

"Jaaaake," she groaned.

"Answer me, Taylor."

She stopped staring at the tabletop and turned her gaze back up to his.

Her big brown eyes were like a window into her soul. They shone as black as obsidian, sparked with fire, as if they too had been born from the belly of a raging volcano. Her nostrils flared and her teeth bit into that pouty lower lip that he wanted to bite and suck and feel all over his body.

"Yeah, I guess," she said tightly, as if the words were being pulled out of her.

"With one or two or three?"

Her eyes darted around the restaurant again. "One or two or three what?" she practically snarled, not quite able to follow the thread of the conversation with his fingers playing dangerously close to her very empty, very aching, very wet pussy.

A squeeze of his hands brought her gaze back to his. "Fingers, Taylor. How many fingers did he fuck you with?"

She looked curiously intrigued by the question. Her breath was starting to pant just that little bit out of control, her arousal growing right before his eyes. "Ooone," she shivered, licking her lips. "Just one."

Well, hell, no wonder it had hurt. She'd never really been prepared—hadn't been stretched to make room so she could enjoy herself. Not that she could've enjoyed herself with Mitch. No, her pleasure was going to be all for him. Always with him. "And what about oral sex?"

Her expression showed equal parts fascination and horror. "What about it?"

His voice went tight. "You didn't even get dripping when he went down on you?"

She opened her mouth to answer at the same time he pushed his thumbs between her tightly clenched thighs, brushing against the soft mound of her curls, just above her clit. A ragged, shuddering moan escaped instead. She swallowed, tried again. "He, um, I mean we never did anything like that. Mitch was never really all that interested in foreplay — at least not with me."

She looked up at him, her eyes dark and hungry, as if she were thinking about giving him head. Maybe imagining having his own face shoved between her legs while he sucked on her pussy. God, he could sixty-nine with her for days on end and never get his fill.

"Do you, um, like doing that?" she whispered, amazed she was asking him such an intimate question.

His thumbs pressed lower, squeezing against either side of that hard, pulsing little bud. He wanted to take it between his lips and flick it with his tongue, over and over and over. "I'm going to love doing it with you. We're going to do everything there is, Taylor. Every sweet little inch of your body is going to be mine. You want that, don't you?" he demanded. "You want it just as badly as I do."

Man, his voice sounded like something you'd hear coming out of a werewolf in some horror flick. All deep and growling and raspy. He was so turned on he was amazed he hadn't shot his load in his pants or busted through his fly — yet.

Her lips trembled. Her eyes hazed. "What — what are you doing to me?" Her nails bit into the skin of his wrists, but instead of pushing him away, she was holding him to her, pressing him down for more. "Oh, God, what are you doing?"

Sandy was going to get one helluva fat tip for giving them this private corner hidden from everyone's view. Taking advantage of their secluded surroundings, Jake stroked his thumbs closer, pressed harder, squeezing. "Haven't you ever touched your clit like this, Taylor? Pressed down right here and made yourself come?"

She whimpered like she was in pain, but he knew it was sexual agony she suffered, not physical. He could smell the sweet, musky scent of her arousal and wanted to delve lower, deeper, where he knew she'd be dripping with juices for him, creaming herself. But he didn't trust himself. He'd have her laid out on the table with his face shoved in her cunt before he knew what hit him, drinking her down his throat like fine wine, eating his fill.

"I—" Her eyes squeezed shut, her bottom lifting off her chair, trying to get more. "I've tried, but it's never felt like this," she groaned in a hoarse whisper, gritting her teeth against the urge to scream. "I thought there must be something wrong and I—Oh, God—I'm on fire!"

"You're pure fucking dynamite, sweetheart." And it was true. Her natural sensuality must've scared the hell out of Mitch. He hadn't been man enough to handle it, not to mention the fact he'd been the wrong man!

Her thighs started shifting, moving apart to allow him more room to explore, and Jake knew it was far past time to get her the hell out of there. Her eyes were wide now, glazed, as if she were on the verge of discovering something wonderful. Any second now she was going to come, but he wanted her alone when she did. He wanted to be able to taste her cream on his tongue. Wanted her to be able to scream with it and lose control. He wanted it all, every little action and reaction. Every little detail and moment with her for the rest of his life.

He just had one more question, but first he withdrew his thumbs and soothed her restless reaction with a gentle sweep across the tops of her legs. He couldn't think about the fact they were parted and she was wet or he'd be under the table and lapping her up without giving a damn who could see.

At the loss of his touch, she looked like someone had just told her she had only seconds to live. For one horrified moment, he thought she might even start to cry, but she took a ragged breath, and he could only admire the way she went straight and regal before him, the Faerie Queen in all her glory. She didn't ask why he stopped, but he told her anyway. "We need to get the hell outta here. My hotel, okay? Right now."

She threaded her fingers through her long hair, still struggling with her breathing. "Uh, yeah. Okay."

He signaled for the check. Before Sandy came back around the corner, he had that last question to ask. "One more question, sweetheart."

Her eyes flew to his. "We've established that Mitch didn't fuck you worth shit. But what about the others?"

Her brow creased. "What others?"

Ah hell, that was what he thought. "You've never gone to bed with anyone else, have you?" he pressed, needing to know.

"Well, no," she said carefully, as if he should've been able to figure it out for himself. "I didn't see the point since the only man I, um, wanted wasn't here."

God help him.

Chapter 6

The instant the door clicked shut behind them, her bags were tossed into the nearest corner and Jake was all over her. One second she was standing in the shadowy moonlight spilling through the curtains, staring at the king-sized bed already turned down fresh for the night, and in the next her feet weren't even touching the floor.

He trembled as he lifted her, her back to his front, his steel-roped arms binding around her, holding her to him. Taylor's head fell back against his left shoulder, her body arching back against his own in offering. With his right arm securing her waist, his left hand snaked across her chest so he could fill his palm with the soft swell of her perfect breast.

Then he stopped.

Jake just held her — savored her.

He enjoyed the moment of the intense, soul-deep satisfaction of finally having the woman he loved right where he wanted her. He buried his face between her neck and shoulder, breathing in the sensual, erotic scent of her skin. Not perfume — just Taylor — fresh and clean and utterly feminine. He wanted to smell that scent all over his body. Wanted to shove his fingers inside of her and feel the musk-sweet moisture he could smell in the air coating his skin.

Knowing he wasn't going to be able to take this as slow as he wanted, Jake nudged the aching mass of his cock against her sweet ass and was rewarded by a rough, ragged moan. Thank God. She sounded as desperate as he was—a good thing considering his legendary control wasn't worth shit with this woman. She smashed it to pieces. Turned him into a crazed, pounding beast that wanted nothing more than to shove his cock so far up her cunt she could taste it at the back of her throat.

Taking a deep breath, he prayed for some shred of patience. They'd only have this one first time, damn it, and he wanted it to be perfect for her. He wanted her to come till it hurt.

"God, Taylor." The words were rough, his breathing already fractured. His fingers squeezed around the soft mound of her breast, rubbing the taut bud of her nipple against his palm. "I feel like I'm gonna explode and I haven't even gotten in you yet."

She shocked the hell out of him when her hand reached between them and grabbed hold of his cock through the front of his pants. Tiny explosions of light and color swam before his eyes. Then she squeezed, stroking him through the restricting fabric, and he had to grit his teeth against the instant, blinding urge to come.

This was insane. How did she do it, making him this crazed, when sex had long ago become such a jaded pastime? Something he could go through the motions of— taking what he needed—without ever letting it dig beneath the surface of his skin. Taylor was already so much a part of him, it was as if his electrified senses were experiencing both the rush of pleasure she took from him, as well as that which she gave.

Her thumb reached just beneath the waistband, right behind the top button, and there was the straining head of his cock. She pressed, stroking the broad tip, and Jake jerked as he felt a burst of pre-cum stream from the slit. "Damn it," he growled, wondering if he was about to embarrass himself. "What in the hell are you doing?"

The low, husky voice that answered didn't sound like his Taylor.

"Do you really have to ask?" she moaned, loving the hot, hard feel of him. She wet her thumb with his moisture and moved it around the wide head, fascinated with his dimensions, losing herself in the moment.

"If you don't stop that, I'm gonna come."

Taylor turned in his arms, pressing close, molding their bodies together. "Good," she said with a wonderfully wicked, playful smile, nipping at his chin. "I want you to, Jake. I don't think I've ever wanted anything more."

Jake grabbed her hand on its way back inside his pants, securing both her wrists as he lifted her arms high above her head. "Slow down!"

He winced at the harsh sound of his voice, but she was pushing him, and there was nowhere else to go but right over the edge. And he was terrified that if he completely lost it, he might end up scaring the hell out of her.

Taylor looked up at her captured wrists, and then snapped her angry glare back on him. "I thought this was what you wanted," she all but growled.

His jaw worked as he struggled to stay calm—to stay in control. "To make love to you—yes! But if you start going all wild on me, I'm gonna have your heels behind your ears and my cock crammed up to your fucking eyeballs before you can so much as blink."

She struggled to draw her hands free, high cheekbones slashed with color. "I thought that's what you wanted!"

Jake closed his eyes on a sharp look of pain, then opened them and backed her up until her legs hit the bed and she felt herself being pushed down onto her back. He loomed over her, so big and tall and wide that she felt dwarfed by his powerful size.

"Yes," he hissed through his teeth, "that's exactly what I want. I want to fuck your little cunt so hard you can't walk straight for a week, Taylor. And that's only for starters! But I was trying to be gentle with you — at least for our first time!"

Laid out at the foot of the bed this way, with her feet barely touching the carpet and her hands now pinned down by either side of her head, Taylor felt a savage desperation for anything but gentleness. Panting, nearly mindless with need, she groaned, "You can be gentle later, Jake! God, if you didn't want me like this right now, you shouldn't have teased me like that at dinner! What in the hell did you expect?"

It finally hit him through his haze of lust. She was just as bad off as he was — just as hungry, just as crazed.

Fuck, what an idiot. Here he had the only woman in the world who melted his heart and made his cock literally ache with need dying for him, and he'd been wasting time worrying about scaring her off.

Fool. Idiot. Asshole.

And he didn't waste a moment more.

Jake quickly shifted his grip on her wrists to one hand so he could give her exactly what she wanted, resting his weight on his forearm beside her head. "You want me outta control?" he grunted, shoving her skirt up to her waist with his free hand and ripping the insubstantial blue lace away. "You got it, baby."

And then he was there, his rough calloused hand pressing between her parted legs, invading her juice soaked pussy with the unerring skill of an expert.

Her eyes were shocked wide, holding his dark, heavy-lidded stare as his fingers moved over her. They traced the swollen seam of her lips, delved inside, separating her to skim over the hard crest of her clit and then lower, circling the tiny, creamy hole. She was drenched, soaked, and he moved his fingers until she coated him, all the while holding her wide-eyed gaze. "You're gushing, Taylor. I've never felt anything so juicy before."

She shivered in answer, shifting her legs farther apart, begging with her eyes for more. This! This was exactly how she'd always known it would be with Jake—this hungry desperation for everything he could give her. She felt free. Free and wonderful and greedy for everything his savagely set features were promising her.

His rough fingertips rubbed across her swollen vulva, circling just inside the silky rim. "Just how tight are you, sweetheart?"

Taylor hoped to God he didn't expect an answer, because all she could do was pant and tremble as he began pushing one big, blunt finger up into her, stretching the narrow passage to make room for him. She watched as his eyes squeezed closed, and then shot back open.

"You feel like a hot little clamp, gripping me as hard as it can. Shit," he rasped, beginning to work a second finger alongside the first, unable to believe how hot and sweet her snug inner walls felt stretching around him.

"I'm probably gonna come the second I cram my cock in here."

He finally got them both lodged within the tiny entrance of her pussy, then reached into her as far as he could, amazed at the tight, wet heat of her clinging depths. How in the hell had he ever lived without this? And why in God's name had he stayed gone for so damn long?

"Jake," she whispered, moving her hips against him with a small rocking motion. "Oh God, that feels so good."

He smiled like a devil as he pulled his cream covered fingers out a few inches and then surged back in, loving the way her hot little pussy struggled to draw him deeper. "That's even better, isn't it?"

He did it again, harder this time, and she moaned in the throws of pure ecstasy. "Your cunt likes that, being stretched so wide, touched so deep. You like being fucked by my fingers, don't you, Taylor?"

Something outrageously wonderful was building inside of her. Something fierce and unstoppable, filling her with power, stretching her skin as her body struggled to make room for it. "Yes! Oh, shit, I can't—"

"Oh, yes, you can," he laughed, loving the look of wonder claiming her flushed face. Any second now she was going to fly right over the edge, and it was worth the pain of holding back just to see it. Her hips were jerking up against his hand, his fingers buried deep inside the wet heat of her sticky sweet cunt, feeling the rapid beat of her heart vibrate around them, clenching tighter and tighter. "I bet you'll like three even better."

Taylor cried out as he shoved a third finger into her. It was too much, but the way he was working them in and out of her pussy felt so good, she almost didn't care that it hurt. And then his thumb was stroking across her throbbing clit, flicking it, pressing down—hard—and she didn't care about anything but the scream clawing its way up out of her throat as her entire body seized in pure mindless rapture.

"Jesus Christ," she heard Jake rasp beneath his breath as her neck and back arched like a bow and raw cries began spilling from her throat.

Tears burned the backs of her eyes. She couldn't believe this was her body writhing beneath him; could believe even less how incredible it felt to feel the deep, rhythmic clenching of her pussy around his fingers, the hot cream spilling from her womb. It was heaven, if anything so erotically sinful could be called such a thing. And the man was obviously an expert, touching her in just the right way to keep the blissful sensations going on and on.

When the last mind shattering ripple finally faded, she felt his fingers pull free with a slick, wet suction that should've been embarrassing as hell, but instead made her feel like the sexiest woman alive. She knew she should thank him or kiss him or attack him for more—but it felt too good just lying there beneath him while his fingers continued to pet her, spreading the warm cream she could feel still pulsing from between her lips over her skin.

She didn't even realize she'd closed her eyes till she heard him say, "Taylor, look at me, sweetheart." She thought he might smile at her sweetly, trying not to embarrass her, but there was nothing sweet about the way Jake was staring down at her. His eyes were wild, dark green, fired with need, and there was a small tick throbbing in his clenched jaw.

Oh, man.

His weight was still braced on one bulging arm beside her head, his hand still trapping both her wrists at what should've been an awkward angle now, but felt just fine. She wanted to moan at the loss of his other hand gently stroking her still trembling pussy when it pulled away — but he startled her by sucking his glistening, cum-soaked fingers straight into his mouth.

"What are you doing?" Taylor winced at the croaking sound of shock in her voice, but she couldn't help it. It was so thrillingly intimate, watching Jake suck on her cream, his eyes going dark with pleasure from her taste.

Holding her fascinated stare the entire time, Jake slowly let his fingers slip free. But he couldn't resist licking the remaining, intoxicating taste of her off his skin, collecting it from between his knuckles with wicked flicks of his tongue. She tasted so sweet, so sexy; he just wanted to eat at her for hours on end. Just shove his face into that drenched cunt and lap and burrow with his tongue until he'd swallowed down every drop.

"What am I doing?" he growled, his nostrils flaring at the enticing scent of her juices on his breath. "Something I should've done the first time I ever laid eyes on you, honey. I'm getting my first taste of the one pussy I've always wanted to be mine."

His hand moved back between her legs, collecting more pearly drops of juice and cum on their rough tips, and then he was pressing them to her lips. "Taste them, Taylor. Open up and see how sweet you are for me. It's like honey and strawberries, all sugary and warm, just flowing down my throat. I can't get enough of it, baby. I just want to fucking drown in it."

Her lips parted the barest bit and he pressed inside, stroking her tongue. Her eyes closed on an embarrassed groan, but then she closed her mouth around his fingers and sucked harder. Oh hell. It was the sexiest thing he'd ever seen.

Suddenly everything was happening at once as Taylor felt herself being roughly pushed up the bed. Jake straddled her legs as he made short work of stripping her shirt and bra off. Then his mouth was at her breasts, drawing her nipples tight, sucking with a strong working motion that included his jaws and lips and tongue, taking her in as if he'd eat her whole.

She writhed beneath him. The sucking motions of his mouth shot straight to the core of her pussy, making her flood with need all over again. And all the while Jake's clever hands were working between them, ripping at her skirt and his own shirt. She didn't know how he managed it, when it seemed his mouth had never left her breasts, but then he was pressing down on top of her and she could feel the heat of his body searing against her sensitive skin. She loved the feel of his naked, hair-covered chest, his hard-muscled torso, the long, muscled length of his pant covered legs, and the huge, burning mass of his erection ramming into her belly from behind his fly.

His mouth found hers, their tongues tangling with the lingering taste of her juices, and she almost cried with relief when he growled, "Spread your legs for me."

But he was moving down her body, taking love bites along the way, and she suddenly realized just what he wanted to do to her.

Oh, no—there was no way in hell she could do that right now. Was there? It was too intimate, too tempting, too—too everything!

"Um, Jake, I—"

"Do it, Taylor. Right here, right now, while you know I'm watching you. I want you to do this just for me, babe. I want to see it all, every little pink inch of that beautiful cunt that belongs to no one but me now."

Her thighs shifted, moved the barest bit apart, and he was arrested, kneeling with his knees on either side of her own, his green eyes dark and hungry. She moved her legs a bit more and he shuddered from fucking head to toe.

"That's it," he groaned, his big hands stroking over the satin smooth skin of her hips and her belly, urging her on. "More, Taylor." His voice was gruff with need, stroking her with sensation. "Give me more."

Her knees had separated again to the point where he could slip between. He knelt there; his eyes glued to the heart-stopping sight of her creamy cunt being slowly revealed to him. It was soft and pussy pink and unbearably delicate, dripping wet, glistening in the soft glow of light. His mouth watered, tongue impatient as he waited for her. He wanted her to do this for him — needed to see her offer herself up to him and give herself over. He wanted her complete surrender to this volatile thing that had always been between them, waiting for its time, desperate for it.

"Look at you," he rasped, his voice as shaky as his hands. "You're beautiful, Taylor. A goddess, sweetheart." His hands caught her behind her knees, urging them higher, pushing them out at her sides. Then he caught her hands where they twisted in the sheets and pulled them between her legs. She panted, twisted, as if she didn't know whether to follow him or bolt in panic.

Jake placed her fingers against the puffy lips, holding them there with his own when she would've pulled away. He knew her eyes were probably wild, shy, but he couldn't pull his gaze away from the beautiful sight of her spread legs long enough to check. "Don't be afraid of me, honey. You don't ever have to be afraid of me."

A startled laugh escaped her. "I'm—I'm not afraid," she wheezed. "I think I'm, um, embarrassed."

A growl purred its way up the back of his throat as he moved her fingers over slippery flesh, wetting her with it. "Don't be, Taylor. You're so pretty and sexy and small—I swear I've never seen anything like it." His wet fingers pulled away from her own, settling on the sensitive inner surfaces of her thighs, making wet imprints as he held her open. She moved to pull her hands away, but he groaned, "Don't move them. Leave them right there and open yourself for me."

"I can't," she whispered, her head shaking. "I don't-"

"Hell, yes, you do. You want this, Taylor. I can't shove my face in here and eat you out till you open it up for me, baby. And I can't wait any longer." His fingers bit into her tender flesh as he struggled to hold himself back. "Come on, Taylor. Spread your pretty little cunt lips so I can suck on that ripe clit and fill you up with my tongue. I'll fuck you with it till you come all over me, and then I'll cram you so tight with my cock it makes you scream. Now—do it right now!"

Taylor squeezed her eyes shut, threw back her head, and did exactly as he commanded.

"Look at you." His hoarse words tumbled over one another in his need and excitement. "Wider, babe. I want you spread wide open. Like that. Hell yeah. Just...like...that—"

And then he was there. Her back arched hard at the first hot touch of his lips, and then he was everywhere.

Lips, tongue, teeth. There was no part of her left untasted, untouched, unexplored. He licked his way along her swelling lips, over the tops of her fingers, and then delved inside, stroking the sensitive skin of her vulva, lapping up the pearly drops of cream with greedy satisfaction. His thumbs joined her fingers, keeping her spread, and he licked and suckled all that sweet, rosy skin that he'd been waiting for his entire life. No woman had ever affected him this way. This was what he'd always craved...always loved...would've died for. This right here, having Taylor laid out and spread open for him, feeding him with her gorgeous, sopping little cunt.

She was so fucking incredible. Juicy and sweet and clean, gushing for him the way he'd always known she would. Beautiful, hoarse cries were spilling from her throat, her hips lifting against his face, drenching him. He couldn't get enough of it. He closed his lips around the taut peak of her clit and suckled like he had at her nipples. She screamed, flooding with juices, soaking his face and the insides of her thighs. Christ, she was the most responsive woman he'd ever known. And it was just for him. All for him.

Jake replaced the pressure on her clit with the roughly calloused pad of his thumb, stroking it while his mouth moved lower to the tiny opening. He flicked it with his tongue, tasted her heat, and then plunged deep, trying to eat his way through her. It was too good. He couldn't get deep enough into her, couldn't shove his face too close. She was warm and sweet and tight and he knew it was gonna kill him to sink his cock deep inside.

"Jake," she cried out, feeling her body break away from her, and he pushed her right over the edge again with a long, slow thrust, tonguing her pussy the same savage way he'd taken her mouth. She broke. She came in a rush of blinding heat and need, gushing like a ripe peach being squeezed between strong fingers. He drank it all in, savoring the jerking spasms of her body and the strong, rhythmic pulls of her womb trying to draw him deeper.

She came forever, but not nearly long enough. He had to get in her, right now, or he was going to die. With one last, lingering lick, he pulled himself up to his knees and attacked the stubborn buttons of his fly. His cock was so fucking hard, he could barely get the blasted things undone, and the shaking of his hands didn't help. He cursed viciously while he worked them open, and she opened her eyes to watch. Her face was flushed, her beautiful breasts rising and falling with each harsh breath, her lips swollen from his kisses and her own teeth. And her pussy was simply crying for him, begging to be fucked long and hard and deep.

Within seconds he had his khakis and shorts shoved down his hard thighs. His cock sprang forward, pounding red and veined and impossibly huge.

Taylor's eyes shot wide as a strangled sound of need and surprise broke from her throat. The shaft was too long and wide, so incredibly thick, reaching up high into the air, trying to get to her. The wide head was blunt and broad, bigger than a large plum, with scalding streams of pre-cum already escaping from the slit in its tip.

She was fascinated. Mesmerized. Unbearably aroused. Her hand shot out to touch him, needing to know the beautiful display of masculinity was real, but Jake caught her wrist, giving a hard shake of his head to warn her not to do it.

Not now, for God's sake, not now, or he'd explode all over her before he ever got inside. And he wanted inside. Hard and fast and deep.

Taylor licked her lips, her eyes shifting from his wicked erection to his fierce expression, and back to his cock again. She shifted restlessly. Moaned. There was a huge sense of emptiness within her that she knew he was about to fill. Her pussy seemed to gasp in need, quivering, begging him to fill her up. Every muscle in his huge body was delineated, his skin hot and sweat-covered, and he was about to become a part of her. She wanted to scream in ecstasy and run and hide all at the same time.

Jake closed his eyes, struggled for some kind of control, only to realize there was no hope of finding it. His cock wanted what it wanted and it was going to take it right now, no matter what. Before she could draw her next breath, he had her legs pushed high and wide, his hands wedged under her knees, holding her in place.

She couldn't move, couldn't scream, and then the hot head of his cock was nudging against her slit, forcing its way inside.

Taylor didn't even realize she'd closed her eyes again until he grunted, "Look at me, Taylor. Now, damn it!"

Her eyes shot open just as the head popped fully into her, stretching her to the point that was both a burning pain and a savage pleasure, but he didn't push any further. He stared down at her, looking violent and wild, and gritted the words through his teeth. "Tell me you want this, Taylor. I don't want to hurt you, but you're so fucking tight and small and all I can think about is pounding you apart."

He pushed a fraction deeper, as if he couldn't help himself, but there were still too many inches to go. Taylor looked down her body to where they joined, watching the way his cock stretched her open. His thick flesh was throbbing and flushed, penetrating an opening far too tiny to ever take it. She figured he was afraid he was going to hurt her, but she wanted him to lose control and shove that brutal, beautiful thing inside of her.

She wasn't stupid; she knew there was going to be some physical pain simply because he was so huge, but she also knew there'd be more of that mind-blowing pleasure. And she wanted more of it, as much as Jake could give her. Her body was demanding it, and Jake looked desperate to comply.

It was the most amazing feeling in the world to know she'd brought him to this state of need. That she, homely little Taylor Moore, was about to make Jake Farrell lose control.

And she knew just how to do it.

She stroked the side of his hot face, cupping his cheek, and smiled up at him. His body went so tense she was amazed he didn't shatter from the pressure. Feeling wicked and naughty and full of life—full of Jake—she pressed her thumb into his mouth, stroking his tongue, while her other thumb brushed his left nipple. He trembled, shuddered, and made a savage noise in the back of his throat that should've scared the hell out of her.

But she wasn't afraid. She never could be. Not of Jake. He owned her heart and her body and her love, and she was about to set him free. With the head of his cock wedged tight inside her pussy, his big body poised atop her, waiting to unleash a desire she never could've even imagined, she swallowed her shyness and said the words she'd never in all her life thought she'd have the courage to say except in her dreams. "Fuck me, Jake. I need you to fuck me as hard as you can, right now."

His face went dark, his expression stunned, as if he were terrified of what she'd just unleashed. But it was too late. Hell, it'd been too late the moment he had set eyes on her. Hearing her tell him to fuck her was every raunchy, lust-driven fantasy he'd ever had turned into an earth-shattering reality. He couldn't resist it. He flexed his hips and drove into her in one hard lunge, breaking her open, hammering his way to the root, so deep his balls were jammed up tight against her ass.

Taylor screamed, arms flung wide from the force of the impact, and felt her pussy pull open around him, then clench tighter with a violent grip, squeezing the huge length of his buried cock so hard he'd probably be bruised.

"Oh, shit. Fuck...fuck...fuck—" he cursed and groaned and shouted as he pulled out and rammed back into her over and over, driving every hot inch of his thick flesh into her as if he could shove himself straight out the other side. He pressed her into the mattress, shoving through the fist-tight clench of her cunt, nearly mad with the wonder of having her under him, being inside of her, feeling her squeeze him tighter than any fist or mouth ever could. His cock was drenched in scalding heat and the clinging depths of her womb. The head rammed past her cervix with every deep thrust until he thought he'd die from the indescribable pleasure of fucking her.

He wanted to come.

Shit, he had to come or he was going to kill himself. They were pounding their way up the bed, moving higher until he had to brace one hand against the headboard to protect her head from banging into it. Then she smiled up at him and his heart burst with the love that he'd held for this woman for so damn long.

He pressed his big body down on hers while his hips jack hammered between her legs — faster, harder, deeper — and kissed her with his juice-covered lips as if his very life depended on it.

His tongue arrowed to the back of her throat and she kissed him back, greedy for her taste on his skin. She was just as desperate, just as wild, sucking on his tongue until he shouted into her mouth. Sweat flew from their heat-soaked bodies, their breathing ragged and frantic, while cock and cunt went at one another like frenzied beasts. He crammed her full, growing bigger with each ramming thrust, forcing the tight channel of muscle to make room for him again and again.

This wasn't sex. He'd had sex hundreds, probably even thousands of times, and it didn't come anywhere close to this. No, this was an absolute possession. A battle to claim the only woman he'd ever loved. He lunged, she tightened, he crammed himself deeper, and she sucked him harder. "Fuck!" he cried against her lips, the words broken and choppy, barely human. "You blow my mind, Taylor. You...blow...my... fucking...mind!"

And she broke. Crashed. Went soaring over the edge, swept off into the sea, her body tumbled and wrecked by the battering force of the waves. Jake watched as her face went blood red, her breath suspended, and then she screamed as a raging orgasm ripped through her, powerful and violent and beautiful. He pressed his mouth to hers, drank in the erotic sounds of her release, and pumped himself into her in a long, pounding stream of hot cum that drained him of pain and filled him with a burning hope for the future.

A future that belonged to no one but them.

Chapter 7

Jake had just claimed the woman who'd forever owned his heart—and now she owned his soul.

The orgasm poured from his body till he thought he'd pass out from the pleasure, so strong it was nearly agony. Whatever he'd experienced sexually in his life before this moment in time was wiped clean from his memory, obliterated from existence, as if he'd only just discovered the carnal wonders of the flesh.

He'd always known on some level that making love to Taylor was going to change him, but he hadn't realized just how drastically he'd be affected. He'd fucked her so hard it'd nearly done him in, but at least he'd have died happy with a smile on his face.

Come hell or high water, he was going to spend the rest of his life buried deep in this woman and never look back—never so much as even think about another body beneath his own. Just the thought of going to bed with anyone but Taylor left him cold. And she was going to know it. Everyone was going to know it.

It wasn't even something that she'd asked for, but it was hers. He was going to be the most faithful, satisfied bastard on the face of the planet till the day he died.

When the wracking spasms finally slowed, he collapsed against her. She grunted as her legs got trapped between them, so he shifted, helping her to lower them to her sides, and then collapsed against her again. Ahhh, yeah, that was perfect. They sealed together, his cock still buried deep inside of her slowly pulsing cunt, and now her pretty little tits were smashed against his chest. He moaned like a man in a cloud of bliss, floating above the world and too happy to worry about how he was ever going to get back down.

She felt it too. He knew she did. She was making sweet, purring sounds in the back of her throat, sighs of bliss and satisfaction, stroking his back with her soft, cool palms, gentling him like an animal.

"Hey, are you okay?" he whispered against the dainty shell of her ear, nuzzling her soft skin with the tip of his nose. It was still difficult to speak, his lungs still aching from the force of his breathing, but he needed to hear her voice.

"Um," she sighed, sounding completely spent.

His lips trailed across her sensitive skin, pressing kisses along the delicate line of her jaw. He smiled at the husky response, knowing she'd found the same incredible heights in his arms that he'd found in hers.

In the perfection of the moment, he remembered the first time he'd ever seen her, just a scared little thing on her first day at a new school, so shy and quietly serene.

It was a small town, small enough that any "new" kid made news, and when that new kid was someone like Taylor—well, she'd made a bigger impact than most. He recalled how he'd been out with the rest of the Varsity football team, running laps around the track before afternoon practice, when he'd seen her cutting across the back of the school on her way home after that first day.

She'd been wearing some kind of sundress, and the wind had whipped it around her legs while the afternoon sun burned bright behind her, setting the soft lines of her body into an intoxicating picture of sensuality. Without even really thinking about it, acting purely on instinct, he'd pulled away from Mitch and the other guys and jogged over to her.

She'd turned at the sound of someone behind her, her big brown eyes opening wide when she caught sight of him walking up to her. "Hey," he'd drawled, stopping when she stopped. "I'm Jake. Jake Farrell."

She hadn't answered, just stood there with a stunned, kind of guarded expression on her pretty face, those big eyes traveling slowly from the top of his sweat soaked head down to his big, Nike covered feet. Then she'd licked her bottom lip, just a quick, innocent flick of her tongue, and he'd felt an answering twitch in his gut the likes of which he'd never experienced. They'd stood staring, lost in each other, he didn't know for how long, until he'd finally cleared his head enough to smile and say, "And you would be Taylor, right? Taylor Moore, isn't it?"

She'd dragged her eyes off the long length of his mostly bare legs, back up to his face, and those pretty lips of hers had lifted into the sweetest smile he'd ever seen. It'd seemed to shoot straight to his heart, right down to the core of his cock, and for the first time in his entire life, he'd had to mentally struggle against his body's demand to go instantly hard within his running shorts. He'd already had more than his fair share of girls—hell, he'd had any girl he'd ever wanted—but nothing in his sexual experience had ever hit him like the sight of Taylor's smile.

"Yeah," she'd replied, "I'm Taylor."

It'd taken him a moment to realize that was all she was going to say, and when she shifted uneasily, her cheeks going pink while he just continued standing there like a bolt-struck idiot, he'd known she was the one. Everything inside of him — things he hadn't even realized were there — had screamed out that this girl was going to be special to him…to his life…in more ways than his adolescent, hormone-raging mind could ever imagine or conceive.

"Listen," he'd said in a sudden rush, "it's Friday night and there's a big ol' group of us that get together at Dixie's Diner over on Lincoln Street. If you're not doing anything, I could pick you up later, take you out to meet some people."

Her doe-like eyes had gone even wider at his words, her bottom lip pulled between her teeth in an innocently seductive action that had made him want to moan. "Look, I know you don't know me or anything, but I swear I'm not a creep."

He knew he'd been rambling, but he'd been too stunned to be his usual laid-back self, too dumbstruck with want to use his usual lines on her. And to be honest, he really hadn't thought they'd work on her anyway. "What I'm trying to say is that you'll be safe with me, I swear. We could just go out and give you a chance to get to know everybody."

She'd opened her mouth to speak, her answer right there on the tip of her pretty little pink tongue, but he'd never got to hear it. At that moment, Wanda and her group of girlfriends had started catcalling behind him, and he'd turned around to tell them to get lost. And when he'd turned back, Taylor was gone, already having disappeared around the far side of the bleachers. He'd started to go after her, and then stopped himself, his ignorant male pride not wanting it to look like he was running after the "new" girl, and it'd been the biggest mistake of his life.

That weekend, Mitch had tracked her down, taken her out for ice cream sodas in town, and by Monday, their fate was set. Mitch's plan had been put into motion, and Jake had never asked her out again. Hell, he'd barely ever had two civil words for her after all the crap Mitch had come back to him with, and God only knew what he'd told Taylor.

So many years wasted because of that jackass, not to mention his own stupidity. But he finally had her where he wanted her, and it was so much sweeter than anything he'd ever known—ever imagined. It was perfection. Pure, hot, sweet perfection.

Suddenly, the words he longed to say rushed up at him from the depths of his soul, but he knew the timing was all wrong. Why in the hell hadn't he controlled himself long enough to tell her about the books? He couldn't go spouting on about his reasons for being here now, not when she was still crammed full of him, swimming in his cum.

Hell, she'd never buy it; much less believe that he'd already been working up the courage to come back for her. Even if he hadn't stumbled across his eye-opening find, he wouldn't have been able to hold out much longer. Shit, staying away from her for as long as he had had nearly driven him outta his fucking mind. And if he'd had to, he'd been more than ready to come back and fight Mitch for her. Divorce or not, he still wanted to kick the bastard's ass.

No matter the obstacles, he wouldn't have given up. So why in the hell hadn't he said all this when he had the chance?

Jake was still trying to come to grips with what she did to him and his utter loss of control, when she shifted beneath him. Knowing he must be crushing her, he gently pulled out of the moist grip of her clinging pussy and rolled to his back, reaching out to pull her possessively into his side.

But Taylor was already rising to her knees, facing him at his hip, mesmerized by the wealth of masculine beauty laid out before her. She wanted to taste every inch of his sun-bronzed skin.

Wanted to learn all the textures and flavors.

Wanted to take sensual bites of all those long, bulging muscles.

The hunger was so great inside of her she could barely hold it in. It pulsed through her blood, pumping against her skin, trying to break free.

"You're beautiful," she rasped, giving him no warning of what was to come next.

One moment she was staring at him as if she'd eat him alive, and in the next her soft sweet lips were wrapped around the wet head of his cock, her tongue rooting into the slit to taste, and Jake felt an inhuman sound of arousal surge from the back of his throat. It was pure animal, primitive and base. His back bowed as his hands found her hair, holding her to him. Her jaws opened wider, drawing him in, and he could've sworn he saw stars explode in his mind in a kaleidoscope of colors.

"Fuck—" he cursed beneath his breath, feeling another wave of cum gather in the root of his cock. He was going to explode right into her mouth, hot and scalding and strong. There was no help for it; he only hoped he didn't scare the hell out of her when it happened.

His hand shot between her legs, fingers searching deep to find her dripping down the insides of her thighs, creaming for him. She was melting, all liquid and warm, and knowing she was getting off on giving him head only intensified what was already the most amazing experience of his life. He struggled to hold back the flood until he'd rolled them to their sides, positioning her so he could lock into her cunt as deeply as she was locked on to him.

He spread her legs, draping one smooth thigh over his shoulder, and then he was eating his way to heaven—just a burning mass of need and desperation for every tender, swollen inch of her gushing pussy. It was crying for him, begging to be eaten again, and Jake answered its pleas with his strong, wicked tongue and warm lips. He sucked, probed, giving her head as if his very life were drawn from this tiny opening and pretty pink flesh that finally tasted of both their juices. How many years had he spent waiting for this moment, living for it, longing with hungry anticipation for the pure perfection of joining with her in a tangle of sheets and skin and erotic flavors?

Her clit, lips, vulva—everything fell under his sensual command, and all the while she was locked on to his cock in a hungry rhythm guaranteed to make his eyeballs roll back into his head. It was so good it was driving him mad, and he had to clench every muscle in his long, hard body to keep from exploding. The need to come called, demanded, while he struggled to last as long as he could, not wanting the exquisite intimacy to end too soon.

It wasn't easy for her, he could tell. She was too new to it, but he loved her eager inexperience all the more. She tried everything she could think of, twirling her tongue around the wide, sensitive head, and then licking along his thick, vein-ridged shaft, before greedily sucking him deep inside the moist cavern of her throat once more. Oh, shit. He drew the ripe, near to bursting bud of her clit between his teeth, wickedly working it with the flat of his tongue, stroking it roughly, determined to bring her first. The instant he felt her climax pound against his face, her syrupy sweet cream bathing into his mouth, he lost it.

She was working to draw him deeper, and Jake couldn't help the surge of his hips as he pushed into her, filling her mouth with his pounding flesh. He was worried it was too much for her, but she didn't try to pull away. He almost cried as she dug her hands into the firm muscles of his ass, pulling him to her, and it *was* too much. His hips thrust while he shot himself against the back of her clinging throat in a powerful stream. She made a startled sound of shock, nearly choking, and then he could feel her mouth working and knew she was eagerly swallowing down every drop. It was so outrageously sexy, coming down her throat; he just kept going and going, unable to stop the surging flow.

When the last drops of warm, salty fluid finally pulsed free, she released the tight suction of her mouth and cleaned him with slow, soft strokes of her tongue.

It killed him. It was too sweet, and he felt the hot tears that had been burning behind his eyes spill free. She licked his balls, the length of his sensitive shaft, and pressed the sweetest of kisses to the tip of his still hard cock, as if thanking him for being so insatiable.

And all the while he cried silently into her cunt, lapping at the glistening, warm drops of cream sliding from her body, wondering how in the hell he'd ever survived without her.

Wondering how he'd find the will to go on if this weekend didn't end the way he planned.

And wondering what it was going to take to convince her to finally follow her heart, instead of her mind.

Chapter 8

They nuzzled and sighed and held tight to each other, their bodies twisted awkwardly atop the wrecked cotton sheets. When Jake had regained some modicum of control, he surrendered gracefully to the lust still roiling through his blood. They were already two fantasies down with thousands to go, but he decided on one of his favorites for their next tumble into the sublime.

Standing beside the bed on wobbly legs, he leaned down and scooped Taylor's still trembling body into his arms, loving her so much he just wanted to squeeze her tight and tell her in no uncertain terms that she wasn't ever getting away from him. Not even heaven or hell could keep him away from her now.

But Taylor's strength of character was too strong, almost as strong as her heart was fragile, and he was too much in love with her to risk it. Which left him where at this point? Keeping her at his sexual mercy, pulsing with pleasure until she conceded they were made for one another and gave him what he wanted? And what he wanted was the promise that he'd never have to live another day of his life without her. Never fall asleep without her warm little body draped over his skin. Never wake up without her lying beside him, soft and sweet and sexy, waiting to share her day and her body and her love. God, he wanted it so bad he could taste it just as clearly as he could taste the lingering sweetness of her cream on his tongue.

She wrapped her arms around his neck as he carried her through the now watery darkness, the first burst of a violent rainstorm beginning to beat a seductive rhythm against the far wall of windows.

"Where are we going?" she mumbled sleepily against his neck, loving the way his naked body felt against her own as he moved, muscles shifting and bunching in a provocative, masculine dance beneath the silky, hair-covered skin. There was a smile in her voice as she added, "I seriously hope you're not thinking of walking out of this room, because we're both still naked."

"Yeah, I know," he whispered gruffly, leaning down to scrape his teeth along the sweetly sensitive tendon that connected her neck and shoulder. He shifted her in his arms, rubbing skin against skin. "I'm not likely to miss a thing like that, honey, especially when it's your sweet little body all naked and soft in my arms."

With one hand, he grabbed a bath towel and shook it out over the cold bathroom counter, protecting her precious backside from the cold tiles as he sat her down. He kept her within the circle of his arms though, afraid she'd bolt once they stopped making physical contact. Instead of blinding them with the bright fluorescent overhead, he flicked on the dim night light, casting the nude angles and planes of her body in a shadowy glow, accentuating the delicate slopes and curves.

As a male animal, Jake had always appreciated the beauty of a woman's body, the wonderfully evocative differences that set it apart from a man's. And he'd held more than a few beautiful figures against his own over the years, taken what temporary comfort he could find in the physical release they were willing to offer, but none had ever affected him the way Taylor's fey little form did.

There was an inherent perfection to Taylor that called to him on every level as a man. He didn't know how to explain it, but it'd always been there, binding and unbreakable, strong enough to survive betrayal and separation and years of agonizing hopelessness. It was emotional, spiritual, and most definitely physical. And now that he knew exactly what it felt like to become a part of her, to mount her and penetrate her and fuck her delicate little cunt into heart-stopping oblivion, he hungered for it the way a zealot sought the divine.

She was no longer a want, but a necessity.

No longer a hunger, but an addiction that demanded to be fed.

She stared up at him in the soft light and shadows, her big brown eyes wide and watchful. She didn't know what to expect from him, and Jake wondered if it was best to keep her guessing, at least until he'd had a chance to prove himself. But he still didn't have a clue how to do it! He'd told her to pack her bags that morning, but she'd brought only one small case and a brown art satchel.

She'd packed for a weekend, not a lifetime.

That meant he had but a handful of days to convince her that what he wanted from her was a forever, as in till death do them part, without exception, instead of a quick sexual fling to get an old itch scratched. And there was no better time to start than now.

She opened her mouth, but he silenced whatever she was going to say with a deep, hungry thrust of his tongue, eating at the sweet, moist cavern like a man—well, like a man starved for the taste of the woman he loved. His hands found her breasts again, the large, calloused palms swallowing the graceful mounds, massaging and reshaping them until she moaned into his mouth.

Then his long fingers dipped inside of her, collecting her cream and his own. He'd filled her up when he came into her, and for the first time in his life, he'd loved tasting himself in a woman when they'd sixty-nined. It was just another act of possession, a way of claiming her, putting his mark on her, and he hungered for it, craving the way they tasted together. He broke the kiss and brought his fingers greedily to his mouth, licked them clean, and knew he needed more.

"Shit, I can't wait," he grunted, pressing her back against the glass. He pushed her knees wide and bent down, shoving his face straight into the dripping pink folds of her pussy, rooting with his tongue for more of their flavor.

"God, Jake," she cried, twisting beneath him, feeling wide open from the physical force of his big hands keeping her spread while his mouth ate at her like he was starved, all lips and tongue and teeth, driven by a primal hunger. "Just—oh, at least let me shower first."

"No," he growled into her, "not yet. I like you like this, all sticky and sweet with cum." His tongue lapped, her body answering his deliciously carnal demands by filling his mouth, flooding his face with cream. "Fuck, you're sweet," he grunted, shifting his head for a better angle. "I can't get enough of it."

"Jake," she half laughed, half moaned, gripping handfuls of his silky black hair, unsure if she was going to push him away or pull him closer. "Jesus, Jake, no one can taste that good. At least let me get clean again first."

"I told you, not yet," he ordered roughly, though the sound was muffled by her throbbing flesh.

She just stared down at him in wonder, fascinated by the sight of his dark head buried between her pale thighs, almost afraid of where he was pushing her with the pleasure he was forcing through her body. Something inside of her was changing, evolving—like a big sleeping cat waking from its nap, stretching to consciousness in the warm afternoon sun.

She was very much aware of the fact that she was becoming physically addicted to Jake Farrell. That was bad. It was dangerous enough to have given him her heart so long ago, and now he was claiming her body too. She'd already lost the emotional battle—how in the hell was she going to find the strength to win the physical one? Where was she going to find the will to fight them both?

Her fingers tightened and she tried to thrust him away.

Jake looked up at her from beneath his lashes, his eyes dark and feral, his mouth wet and glistening. "Don't make me stop," he whispered, his voice ragged and on edge, and she wondered if he felt it too, this dangerous connection binding them together, interconnecting their lives until it was difficult to tell where one ended and the other began. "Please, Taylor. You taste so sweet. Like us. Like fucking. Don't make me stop."

Uh-oh. Too late.

The need opened up, huge and gaping, demanding to be filled, and her fingers tightened, pressing his head back down, pulling his face into her pussy while a raw cry of need rushed past her lips.

Rhyannon Byrd

His eyes closed, and he ate again, burrowing his tongue into her opening, cupping her ass in his hands to lift her higher, going and going until her world was turning black and her lungs were aching for air. The climax ripped through her, somehow stronger than the others, a violent force of love and physical awareness that started in the clenching muscles of her womb and spiked through her body, hard and fast and pounding, as painful as it was sweet.

And then he was there, his big arms wrapping around her, his cock huge and hot and hard as granite, pushing against her still quivering slit. His fingers speared into her hair until she could feel the imprint of each one against her scalp, and he held her still as his mouth came down on hers the same instant he rammed back inside. He used the counter to brace her while his thick cock just kept going, filling her still pulsing pussy one beautiful, heavy inch at a time.

Sweat poured from his body, his muscles cramping as he struggled to keep it together. No—he was going to come too soon. He was too on edge, too turned on.

With a low curse, Jake pulled out of her sweet, clinging depths before he'd even fully made it inside, stumbling back against the wall, staring at her as if he didn't quite know what to make of her.

Where in the hell had his legendary control gone—the one that kept him screwing for hours, wringing pleasure out of his partners until they passed out in exhausted satisfaction? Huh! All he had to do was look at Taylor and he was ready to come like some short-triggered boy of sixteen. If he weren't so fucking in love with her, he'd have found it humiliating as hell.

Then Taylor moved gracefully off the counter and dropped down on her knees in front of him, staring up at his cock with a look of hungry desperation burning in her big brown eyes.

Oh, hell.

Her lips parted, tongue flicking daintily against her bottom lip, and his cock twitched, jumping into the air, bringing a smile to her mouth. Then she leaned forward and flicked the big, wet head with her tongue and his damn knees nearly gave out.

"Mmm," she moaned, licking her way down the side of his cock. "You're right, Jake. We do taste good together."

That was it. Jake gripped the root of his massive erection, clamping down tight to stop the flow of cum, gritting his teeth as he fought for some shred of control. He breathed through his nose, the sound rough and deep, like a raging bull while the air surged hard and heavy through his lungs.

Taylor watched him struggle with a sense of awe. He was so impossibly sexy and rugged, rippling with muscle, looking down at her with a fierce expression that was equal parts stunned disbelief and blistering lust. Everything about the man was a seduction. He was just so masculine, so dangerous, so elementally male. His dark hair and hungry green eyes and sun-kissed skin were a dramatic contrast against her own pale coloring, so that it looked as if his golden body actually glowed before her with heat and vitality.

She licked her lips, swaying with need. And then she was being lifted against his front, her legs moving instinctively to straddle his waist, and his thick cock was working its way back up inside of her once more. It pushed through her in a powerful, insistent thrust, filling her empty, aching pussy till she thought she'd bust open around him.

"I thought—" she panted, trying to form a coherent sentence while his hard, hot cock forced the walls of her pussy apart—digging deep—so deliciously deep inside of her. "I mean—I didn't know guys could do it this many times."

His lips broke into a warm, sensual smile as he walked her across the floor to the enclosed shower in the corner of the small room, both of them gasping from the friction as he moved. "Taylor, I've only fucked you once and come twice. No way in hell is that enough. I'm not anywhere close to being done with you tonight, and then we get to start all over again tomorrow."

She squirmed in his arms. "Aren't you sore?"

"Yeah, my cock feels kinda bruised from being squeezed so tight, but trust me—it feels better in than out." His clever tongue licked the shell of her ear, dipping inside, his breath warm against her skin. "But what about you? I rode you pretty hard, sweetheart, and you're really swollen. Can you take me again, because I sure as hell can't promise to go any easier on you this time around?"

"Isn't it a little late to be asking that question?"

His face looked pained, his voice barely human as he growled, "Do you want me to stop?"

She sought his mouth for another kiss, groaning against his silk-textured lips. "I'm tender, but you're right—it feels better in than out."

Jake pushed the door open behind her and walked her into the small stall, their mouths never breaking contact, and pressed her body up against the back wall of tiles. Reaching behind him with one hand, he twisted the knob until a blast of ice-cold water slammed into his back. He growled into her mouth, pressing his body closer into hers, sharing her heat, and twisted the knob until the water was streaming hot and hard against his skin, filling the frigid air with steam.

The feel of his wet skin against her own while his cock claimed possession of her pussy, a thick, pulsing mass of flesh cramming her full, nearly brought her to orgasm then and there.

Jake grabbed hold of her slim hips, his fingers biting into her tender flesh, pulled out of the cusp of her opening and gave her a hard, heavy lunge that packed him back in to the hilt, all the way to the root of his cock, slamming her against the wet shower wall, then grinding there inside of her.

He looked down at her through heat and steam, his green eyes burning like twin lights of flame. "Do you have any idea how many times I've been in the shower and grabbed my cock while thinking about you, fantasizing about how sweet it'd be to have you in front of me, all ripe and wet, waiting for me to become a part of you?"

She shook her head, words completely failing her.

With her back braced against the wall and her legs wrapped tight around his waist, his big, rough hands were free to roam and explore. Jake placed them on her shoulders, smoothing the wet tendrils of her hair back, then allowed them to rasp down her chest till he was cupping her breasts, teasing the swollen nipples with the calluses on his palms. "Too many times to count, Taylor. But you know what?"

"What?" she groaned, loving the way he twisted her sensitive nipples between his fingertips, the ease with which he reduced her to a quivering mass of need and want and lust. She hungered for him so badly it was like a living thing clawing at the back of her throat, aching between her legs, mad for the touch and taste of his skin.

He cupped her cheeks, tilting her face up to his, brushing his lips against her wet lashes, the delicate curve of her cheek. "I didn't even come close. Having you here is so much more than anything I could've ever imagined. How do you do it to me, Taylor?" he rasped, biting kisses along her jaw. "How do you make me ache to fuck, needing you so damn bad it feels like I'll die if I don't get back inside of you like this and stay here forever?"

Because I love you.

She couldn't say the words, but she could show him. She pressed against him, all soft, womanly textures, tastes and scents, and wrapped her body around his own. The power rode them, and they struggled against one another, trying to crawl into the other's skin, eager for the other's touch, unable to get close enough.

He reached between them and found her throbbing clit, so near to bursting all he had to do was brush against it with his thumb and her pussy gripped him so tightly he felt deliciously bruised. The water was beating down hard and heavy against his back, her soft hands clutching at him, the innocent touches driving him as wild as the deep, luscious clenching of her cunt, and he pinched her clit between his thumb and forefinger, giving a gentle tug, and then a not so gentle one that had her jerking against him, sobbing into his mouth.

Jake took her bottom lip between his teeth and pulled, just like his wicked fingers were pulling at her clit, and

Taylor swore she almost lost consciousness from the rush of sensation that pierced her. There was a pulsing friction of heat and pounding blood in her veins. He worked her like clay, molding this raging, volatile creature in place of the shy, timid woman who had lived there before.

The power shifted between them. One moment a gentle ebb and flow. The next a violent push and shove. It tumbled over them, around them, sucking them under like a bottomless force of gravity and she broke apart on a rippling wave of love and ecstasy.

With a long, guttural groan, he began coming, grasping the soft, sweet cheeks of her ass, grinding against her, drilling her into the wall. He gritted his teeth as his body seized and jerked, the orgasm burning through him, strong and violent and raging, while the mystery of the petite woman delicately sinking her teeth into his shoulder shifted his entire world on its axis.

Time became lost, dark and jagged. When he finally came back to reality, he was pressing heavily against her with his legs damn near knocked out from under him. His chest hurt from the force of his harsh breathing, and he could feel her small, cool hands stroking slowly down the rigid muscles of his back in a gentle, soothing caress that for some strange reason made his blood roar through his ears as if she were stroking his cock.

Oh man, he had it so bad for this woman. He was crazy fucking nuts for her.

And amazing as it was, considering the force of his release, he was still half hard inside of her and growing harder by the second. He had to be careful or his dick was going to end up killing both of them. Reluctant to hurt her, Jake slowly pulled back his hips, knowing her battered little pussy would need a few more minutes of recovery time before taking him again.

They stayed beneath the spray, gently soaping each other's bodies, both too shaky to risk walking, until the water turned cold. Taylor stood shivering against the shower wall, feeling like she'd just survived a cataclysmic, life-altering experience, and knowing she could too quickly become dependent on this kind of thing on a regular basis.

Huh, she silently muttered, shutting her eyes against the pathetic reality of her situation. *Come off it, Taylor.*

She was already dependent on it, and they'd only been going at it for an hour or so. Who knew what kind of condition she'd be in by the time he packed up and headed back home? He'd probably leave her wrung out and pulsing on the floor, just a sopping mass of cream and cum and tears.

And the worse part was that she knew there wasn't anything she could do to stop it. She was his to do with as he pleased for as long as he wanted. It was a fact. The only thing to do was stick to her original plan and wring as much earth-shattering pleasure from it as she could, while she had the chance, then live off the wondrous experience for the rest of her life.

She tried to convince herself that it was a realistic plan.

It made sense.

It was the smart thing to do.

The only thing she couldn't figure out was what this gorgeous man was doing here with her in the first place.

Chapter 9

Jake's desire to care for her seemed to have no end as he gently wrapped her wet body in a soft, fluffy towel and carried her back to their wreck of a bed. While she watched him with curious eyes, he pulled her brush from her small bag of toiletries and settling himself behind her, slowly began working the tangles from her hair, his strokes amazingly gentle considering his intimidating size and strength.

When he was done, he tossed her wet towel on a nearby chair and pulled her chilled body beneath his own, heating her faster than any blanket or fire ever could. With a wicked, carnal smile, he began kissing his way down her front, beginning with the delicate lobes of her ears, over her throat, treating her puffy pink nipples to slow, wet strokes with the flat of his tongue, and then trailing biting kisses down the center of her stomach straight to the soft, luxurious patch of curls decorating the apex of her thighs.

Then he stopped, and she moaned from the loss of his mobile lips as he rolled her to her stomach, working her body as easily as a doll, repeating the same process on her back. He gave a provocative lick to the sensitive skin across the nape of her neck, then kissed his way down the elegant slope of her spine. Even the cheeks of her ass were treated to gentle, teasing bites, and then he stopped, flipping her back to her front again.

Taylor looked up at him from beneath her lashes, her mind flooding with memories of him as a boy, marveling at the fact that she was here with him like this now—every facet of her being, both emotionally and physically, being ravaged by the powerful man he had become. He was everything she'd always known he'd be...and so much more.

He was devastating—in the truest, most brilliant sense of the world.

"Do you remember the last time we ever saw each other? The night before you left?" Her voice was husky from her earlier cries of pleasure, her limbs feeling deliciously heavy as she raised her hand to sift through the black silk of his hair.

"Yeah, I remember," he rasped, drawing her hand to his mouth.

His lips pressed a tender kiss to her palm, as if he were desperate to place a claim on every part of her.

"I almost hated you that night," she whispered, recalling the torment of finding him screwing Wanda Merton in the backseat of Mitch's car at the drive-in. It'd been just a few weeks after his graduation, and she'd gone on one of those rare outings with her mother, to the movies of all things. She'd been on her way to the restrooms when she'd passed Mitch's car parked four rows behind where her mother had parked their old Chevy.

She still remembered with perfect clarity walking up to the door and opening it, fully expecting to find Mitch screwing around with someone inside, instead of being on the hunting trip he'd claimed to be taking with his dad. But the face that had looked back at her from the backseat hadn't been Mitch's. No, it'd been Jake's, his eyes shocked wide, staring straight back at her while she'd stood there for those stunned seconds, watching Wanda ride him while he sat sprawled across the backseat. She'd wanted to run—to run and find the nearest place to lose the churning contents of her stomach, but her feet had been rooted in place. At least until Wanda had thrown back her head, her long red hair tumbling down her naked back, and let out a bloodcurdling scream while her then thin body had writhed in the throes of ecstasy.

Suddenly she'd been running across the dirt lot, her feet moving without any recognizable direction from her brain—and then Jake had been grasping onto her arm from behind, pulling her around so quickly she'd been thrown against him.

"Get away from me!" she'd screamed, hating the fact that he would see her tears. Hating the fact that she cared what he did and with whom. Hating that it hurt so badly—that she wanted him for her own. She'd lashed out in her fury, pounding her small fists against his sweatshirt-covered chest, struggling to be set free.

"Taylor, damn it, stop it before you hurt yourself," he'd growled, gripping her upper arms so that he could hold her still. His green eyes had been wild as he'd stared down at her in the moonlit darkness, hair tousled from his back seat romp with Wanda, blue jeans hanging onto his hips by sheer force of will, the fly still undone. His cock had been a long, thick ridge beneath the soft cotton of his boxers—her every sense tuned into the fact that he was still hard.

"How could you?" she'd groaned, not knowing where the words tumbling past her lips were coming from, unable to stop them. "How could you do that with *her*, Jake?"

It was bad enough that she'd found him in the act with another girl, when she'd loved him with all the budding passion of a young girl's heart, but the fact that it was Wanda had simply been too much to bear. Wanda, who had systematically tried to make her life a living hell. Wanda, who had spent the entire year trying to turn people against her. Taylor hadn't even known why the captain of the cheerleading squad hated her—she only knew that she did.

Jake's hands had tightened against her flesh, fingers biting hard enough to bruise. He'd pulled her closer, not close enough that they were actually touching, but close enough that he could lean down and look her in the eye, face to face. "What's it to you who I fuck, Taylor?"

She'd swallowed her girlish pride enough to say, "Nothing, Jake. Fuck every whore in town if that's what you want."

His face had tightened, a pained look of need spilling from the deep green pools of his eyes. "What do you know about what I want? You may see me every damn day of my life, but you don't know shit about me." Then his eyes had traveled over her tear-stained face in the softest, most intimate caress, as if he'd touched her with a gentle brush of his lips instead. "You don't have a fucking clue, Taylor."

Then he'd let her go, taken a quick step back away from her, and then another, his big hands clenching into fists at his sides. She'd watched him with anxious eyes, knowing he was trying to tell her something, but too naïve to understand what it was.

And they'd stood there just like that, staring across the moonlit darkness for what seemed like forever, until the car on the low rise above them had started honking its horn for them to move.

"When you talk to him, tell Mitch I'll leave his car at the school," he'd said in a low, hoarse rumble, and with a last sweep of his smoldering green eyes down the length of her body, he'd turned and walked away.

That was the last time she'd ever seen him.

Until today.

And now she lay on her back beneath him, her entire body strumming in anticipation, her skin tingling from the slow burn he ignited, making her simmer. It was an odd feeling, both relaxing and uncomfortably exciting, languid yet expectant, so that it was both a shocking relief and a startling rush of ecstasy when his fingers found her center, two twisting deep into her core, thick and wide, scraping her inner walls with his short nails as he explored the fist-tight sheath.

When he spoke, his voice was a deep rasp of need, honest and sincere. "I remember that night, Taylor. I remember that I wanted you more than anything in the world. More than my own life. I remember almost hating you for wanting you so bad, until it was like a sickness in my gut, pulling me apart. I remember screwing Wanda if for no other reason than to get back at you for not wanting me the same way."

He leaned down, brushing his lips across hers, rubbing the words into them. "I remember thinking of you the entire time I was pounding inside of her, and when I saw you looking in through that open car door, it was like a knife through my heart. I felt so sick and ashamed I wanted to fucking die, so angry and hungry for you I wanted to throw you over my shoulder and take you away from this place forever. Take you anywhere where I could make you mine."

He lifted his face, looking straight into her big brown eyes, knowing that everything he felt was there on his face for her to see, if she'd only look close enough. "I knew that night that I had to go, but I shouldn't have left without you, Taylor. I should have told you how I felt. You *are* mine, and I should have taken you with me. And I've regretted not doing it every second of every miserable fucking day I've spent without you."

Her eyes closed, smooth brow knitted in thought, and his heart sank. He watched as her long lashes lifted, and when she looked back up at him, he knew she wasn't going to acknowledge the words that had tumbled forth from his heart. The words that he wanted to keep saying and shouting again and again until she finally got the message. Until they finally battered down all those damn walls she'd spent the last ten years of her life erecting. Fortifying. Hiding behind.

"What—what made you decide to build houses?"

The sudden, abrupt change in topic was jolting, and he removed his hand from between her thighs with a small sigh, knowing he'd pushed her too far again too quickly. With an inner grimace, he thought about how to answer what should have been a very simple question—but wasn't.

Taylor could tell by his expression that he was weighing his words, deciding on how much to tell her. It was odd, she mused, because his choice of occupations couldn't have had anything to do with her. Maybe it had to do with a woman.

Someone from his past?

Not that she wanted to know about her, but then Jake wasn't likely to go spouting off about some old girlfriend either. He was too much of a gentleman for that—though not so much of one that he didn't completely overpower her with his aggressive, dominant sexuality.

And that was just fine by her, she thought with a luxurious stretch of deliciously well-used muscles, refusing to think about the warm rush of ecstasy his heart stopping words had sent rocketing through her.

Fine and fucking dandy.

His eyes watched the movement of her body as she stretched, following every shift of muscle as she moved with total, almost fixated attention. A long sigh of feminine pride passed her lips, and the corner of his mouth lifted, his hand moving from her thigh to rest heavily upon her stomach.

He rubbed slow circles around her navel, watching the motion of his big, dark hand against her pale flesh, and answered her question. "I knew I didn't want to be stuck behind some desk for the rest of my life, stuffed inside a suit and kissing corporate ass every damn day."

He snorted, shaking his head, and she watched as the movement caused a lock of black silk to fall down across his brow, giving him an even more rakish appearance.

"After I blew my knee out my sophomore year of college, football was out of the question, so I sat back and thought about what was really important to me—what I really wanted to spend the rest of my life doing."

Without meeting her eyes, his hand still making those slow, delirious circles, he added, "Learning to build someone's foundation—maybe even their dream—with my own hands seemed like a fairly meaningful thing to do, though it probably sounds lame as hell."

"Don't do that, Jake," she said, hating to hear him belittle something that had obviously been a very important decision to him. "There's nothing wrong with wanting to give your life meaning. Nothing wrong with it being about more than a paycheck." She smiled, thinking of the brand new full sized truck parked outside the hotel and the fact that he'd repaid his start up loan within his first two years of business. "Though I'm thinking your doing all right in the paycheck department as well."

His index finger dipped into her navel, while his fingers and thumb spread, nearly spanning the width of her stomach. "I can't complain, sugar, but it's not about the money. I need to be out in the sun and the rain and the snow, working with my hands, going till my muscles burn and I'm soaked in sweat. It's grueling, but it's what keeps me sane."

And in such mouthwatering shape, Taylor mused silently to herself. "It sounds just like you," she whispered, finding it ridiculously erotic to watch him watching his hand on her stomach. "Your life—building things that are exceptionally beautiful and strong—that suits you, Jake."

He lifted his head, his glittering green eyes capturing her gaze. "You're beautiful—and strong, but for some damn reason, you just don't know it," he murmured in a husky caress, seducing her with his voice alone.

She would have loved to believe him, but she had to be truthful—at least about this. "I'm not strong, Jake. Not at all."

"You are, Taylor, but you just don't see it. You think I don't know the hell it's been for you to stay here—through your marriage and after? Damn, Taylor, anyone else would've run at the first chance, but you stayed."

She shook her head slightly. "That was just stupid, stubborn pride, Jake—not strength. I've let people walk all over me my entire life."

His brow arched, fingers flexing against the firm muscles of her belly. "And what about when you knocked Jackson Blaine's teeth down his throat at the Winter Wonderland Dance when he came up behind you and grabbed one of your pretty little breasts?"

"He was asking for it, the jerk," she mumbled, unable to stop the blush from spreading across her cheeks. "And I wasn't the only girl who'd had enough of his groping. By the end of the night, someone had given him a black eye to go along with his busted lip."

His mouth twitched, eyes gleaming with a mischievous sparkle. "You didn't," she gasped, though the idea of Jake having stood up for her back then sent a warm feeling through her fluttering stomach that had nothing to do with sex. "If they'd found out, you would've gotten thrown off the varsity team for fighting!"

He gave a masculine snort of outrage. "There wasn't any fight to it. That spoiled little rich kid was blabbering like a baby after the first hit. And," he drawled, his lips lifting in a wicked grin, "your gorgeous, tough little ass already had him shaking in his boots before I even got to him."

She laughed softly, ridiculously pleased by his playful praise, and thinking of how Jake had complimented her more in one night than Mitch had in their entire marriage. But then her laughter became a soft groan as his head lowered, his tongue lapping at her nipples while his fingers moved lower to begin another slow, erotic exploration within her body.

His touch was light and teasing, demanding nothing more than her trust and acceptance. And yet they kept the deep throb of desire at a steady burn, just waiting for the moment when he'd push her over the edge, hurling her back into a full-fledged boil.

It was like a dream—seeing herself like this with Jake Farrell, lying beside him with her legs spread wide, knees bent, and every part of her cum soaked pussy completely exposed.

And she still couldn't believe those were her juices streaming between her thighs. For someone who'd thought she'd never be able to do it right, she'd had no trouble coming like crazy in Jake's arms. Nothing she'd ever read had come anywhere close to showing her what the "real" thing was like. The utter magnificence of sensation. The complete loss of everything you are and know and understand to sharp, delicious, dizzying pleasure.

And now that she'd experienced it, she wanted it again and again. She wanted to feast on them—on him. Wanted to fill herself up until she was so full she overflowed, her blood pounding like a tribal drum while she pumped and writhed and came all over him.

Oh, yeah, a woman could definitely get addicted to this.

After all these years, she finally understood what all the fuss was about.

"Now it's your turn," he said, his warm breath tickling her skin, and she could hear the smile in his voice. "I want you to tell me about your life."

I want you to tell me about the paintings.

Taylor laughed, and though it was a struggle to think straight with his tongue on her nipple and his fingers dipping leisurely into her drenched vagina, she knew not to say too much. She would keep her secrets in their short time together, and be able to walk away with her held high. There was too much of her at risk with this man — giving him the truth about her art would be like giving him everything. Because that was what she'd spent the last ten years painting — her heart's desire.

And what was she doing, lying here beneath his gorgeous body thinking about later? She should be enjoying now! Taking it for everything it was worth! Wringing it of pleasure! Gorging herself on this sensual feast of moans and flesh and never-ending orgasms while she had the chance!

Jake saw the change in her, the powerful rise of need, and his mind went blank. All the questions he'd wanted to ask were lost as physical hunger clawed through him once more, anxious and demanding. One moment they were talking, and in the next, he'd taken his teasing hand from between her legs and was rubbing the cream on his fingers into her pink nipples and parted lips.

"What are you doing?"

"I'm still hungry," he groaned the instant before his tongue licked slowly across her bottom lip, collecting her taste. He growled with satisfaction, doing it again, then allowed his tongue to slip into her mouth, sharing her sweet, erotic taste with her.

Taylor's choked whimper of surprise sent lust pounding through him. The low moan that followed nearly made him come. With infinite time and care, he worked his way down her body, lingering on her damp raspberry nipples, the shallow indentation of her navel, until at last he settled himself back between her wide spread thighs and feasted on her sex-ravaged cunt. It was such a pretty shade of pink, scented like sin, and tasted too damn good to be true. He could spend the rest of his life with his face shoved right in it, feeling it come all over him.

He smiled against her warm, wet skin—then bit down softly on her clit, giving it a gentle tug. Her hips lifted, shoving her pussy in his face, and he laughed a rich sound of boyish delight. "And I might as well torture the answers out of you while I'm busy filling up."

On you.

"Won't work," she quipped, loving this roguish, mischievous side of him that she'd never known was there. She knew he'd always had a good sense of humor with his friends, all his football buddies and the never-ending chain of girls he'd dated, but she'd never been the recipient of one of those teasing smiles herself. He looked up at her, and it was so warm and playful it just made her go all gooey inside, like the dripping decadence of a fresh baked chocolate chip cookie melting between her fingers. "I'm afraid my lips are sealed."

He held her sassy, daring stare while his fingers pushed the wet, swollen lips of her cunt apart, spreading her as wide as she'd go. "They don't feel so sealed to me," he laughed, the masculine chuckle a low rumble of sound, his breath teasing the soft, sensitive flesh. "I'd say you have a real sweet smile going on down here between your silky little thighs."

A girlish burst of laughter escaped her, and she blushed brighter, almost as embarrassed by the giggle as she was by the wicked torment of his fingers playing over her, keeping her held open. It was a decadent feeling to know he could feel her cream against his fingers. To know that any second now he would look back down at her pussy to see how wickedly he'd displayed it for his hot, hungry gaze. And bubbling beneath the dark heat of his sexuality was the joy of laughing and smiling with him, being playful in the bedroom when she'd never thought of sex as something even remotely fun before.

Fun, she mused, rolling the word around in her mind while trying to decide if it was the right one. Kind of strange, but yeah, it fit. Sex with Jake was raw and hungry and powerfully extreme, a complete devastation of sense and self—but it was a hell of a lot of fun too.

There were no two ways about it—this was the best damn time she'd ever had.

And then suddenly his fingers were slipping back inside, stretching her to that point beyond pleasure, and her snug, straining muscles clamped down hard enough to make his breath hiss between his teeth. He knelt between her thighs and used his free hand to grab his cock. Then he gripped himself in his big fist and stroked from the massively thick root, up his long length, to the impressively large, glistening head.

Taylor watched with wide, fascinated eyes as he milked one pearly drop of moisture from the slit. He loved the way she watched his cock, her shy eyes too curious not to look, her expression telling him everything he needed to know. "And it's all yours, honey. All of it."

Just like I'm all yours. All of me.

"Yeah, mine," she whispered, licking her lips in an unconscious gesture of want.

He swiped the warm, salty bead from the head of his cock with his finger and lifted it to her mouth, offering it to her as she levered herself up with her arms. She opened her mouth and her small pink tongue flicked out to lick it off.

His growl was long and low. She answered with her own soft sound of want and arousal, and then opened up and drew his finger completely into her mouth. Her moist heat closed around him. Then she sucked on him. Hard. What little sanity he had left fractured in that instant.

"Take a deep breath and hold on," he ordered roughly, pushing her legs up, folding them over until she was spread out and open in front of him, grasping for whatever part of him he wanted to give her. He felt savagely primitive, on the verge of violence in his need to stake his claim again and again.

With his heart lodged in his throat, he whispered, "You want it?"

"Please, Jake," she moaned. Her hips lifted, offering, begging, and he bent his head to give her beautiful, open pussy one more long, hungry lick.

He pulled back just far enough to give him a nice, up-close shot of the hottest little cunt he'd ever had. He loved its smell, its taste. Loved the way her clit throbbed and her little hole spilled with more of that sweet fucking cream. "This is mine, Taylor. All of it. All mine."

His tongue flicked out to catch the stream of juices slipping from her pink slit, and he smiled at the bite of her nails in the tops of his shoulders. "You know, honey, I just can't decide which I love more—fucking it, or eating it."

"Oh, God." Her voice cracked, and she yelled, "Now, Jake! Just do it! Put it in!"

He'd have laughed at the way she commanded him, shouting like an outraged general, but he didn't have the strength. There was nothing but blinding need as he pressed the deeply flushed tip of his cock against her drenched cunt, nudging the pulsing head between her swollen lips until it penetrated the tiny, quivering mouth hidden within. Bracing himself on his knees, he grasped her hips and lifted her, holding her firmly in his grip.

His voice trembled, shakily with need. "I've never been so hard in my entire life. You drive me outta my mind, woman, right over the fuckin' edge."

"Jake." His name emerged as a moan...a plea...a demand.

He battled against the raging need of his body to take, to plunge his aching cock as far into her as he could go, and took one charged moment to appreciate the beauty of her spread out and open. Vulnerable. Wanting him.

He leaned over her, pressing down on her, and his warm breath found her ear. "I love you, Taylor."

Chapter 10

She went so still beneath him—he couldn't even feel her breathe.

He nuzzled the side of her neck, pressed a tender kiss to her shoulder, feeling the words rush up through him, true and unstoppable. "I'm in love with you." His deep voice emerged gruff with emotion, reverberating through their joined bodies, touching her deep inside. "I've never loved another woman, Taylor. It's always been you. Always. It always will be."

"No!" she cried out, suddenly twisting beneath him, shaking with rage. It was too cruel to hear this now—now, when it was too late for it. Now, when their chance at a happily ever after had so long ago been destroyed by Mitch's malicious lies.

Jake slowly pulled back, an uneasy shock and painful ache burning through his body as he watched her scramble away from him, practically stumbling to the other side of the room.

"Don't...don't ever say that." Her voice was a whisper of sound, hollow and shaky.

Wondering what in the hell was happening, he moved to sit on the edge of the bed. There was a dull thudding in his heart, like something hard and heavy that he couldn't keep from sinking. "I'm trying to be understanding, but I just don't get it, Taylor." His voice was rough, sounding little more than a snarl, and he pushed both hands through his hair, shaking his disheveled head in disbelief as her reaction really began to sink in. "You'll let me fuck you, but I'm not allowed to love you?"

It wasn't possible for her to get any redder, her thin frame quivering; a frail silhouette on the other side of the room. He was suddenly so angry, more furious than he'd ever been before, hating the way she was looking at him, like she was actually horrified by his admission. Appalled by the fact that what he'd said just might be true.

He'd opened up his heart and told her how he felt, and she was throwing it back in his face without even giving him a chance to explain.

Fuck this, he thought, standing beside the bed, all six-foot-three inches of him shaking with rage. "I can fuck you, but I can't love you? Is that it, Taylor? You'll take my cock, but nothing more, honey? You'll let me screw you through the mattress and then send me on my fucking way?"

"Jesus, Jake. What do you want from me?"

"I want this," he shouted, swiping his arm in the air to encompass the wrecked bedding behind him, his mind churning in panic for a way to keep her from bolting on him. "I want this weekend. Anything I say. Anything I want. I want complete access to that beautiful little body of yours from head to toe, and if I can't convince you in that time that I'm serious about wanting you in my life forever, then I'll leave without you even having to tell me to go."

Her arms trembled, so she held them tighter, putting everything she had into this fragile show of strength. Or was it just stupidity? All her options seemed destined for failure here. If she followed her heart, what would happen when he came to his senses or some gorgeous blonde caught his eye and he bailed? But if she followed the dictates of her still pulsing flesh, satiating herself on the decadent pleasure he lavished upon her, would she be any better off when the weekend was over and he drove back out of her life?

Hell no.

Basically, she was screwed no matter what she did. The only difference was that option one left her in a constant state of heartbreaking anticipation, awaiting the god-awful moment of truth—while his outrageous proposal for a weekend full of mind shattering fucking gave her a nice, tidy deadline for the gut wrenching heartache to begin.

"All right. Okay. You can have your weekend, but when it's over you leave, Jake. No arguments. You walk back out of my life as easily as you did the first time. Do we have a deal?"

He moved across the room with the predatory ease of a dangerous jungle cat. She watched him with wide, avid eyes, feeling drunk on his beauty; the long, lean muscles moving beneath his golden skin as lethal to her senses as the blisteringly hot look in his green eyes.

Most women would've probably tried not to be quite so obvious in their fascination, but she couldn't help it. She felt flushed with heat, dizzy with desire, just from watching the gorgeous man walk across a blasted room. Of course, the fact he was still bare-assed naked with his brutally beautiful cock rising high and hard and hungry in front of him—the huge shaft gleaming with *her* juices— might've had something to do with it. Then again, she was just as crazy for him with clothes as without.

That was the thing with love. It made you silly-sick for a person, even when you knew it was going to end up killing you in the end. Kingdoms had been built and destroyed on it since time began—and Taylor knew she was going to be no different. The least she could do was to wring it of as much ecstasy as she could while she still had the chance, and then treasure the memories, holding them to her heart for as long as she could.

It was pathetic, and in that moment, she hated Mitch with such wounded malice that it twisted through her veins, poisoning her blood. She could taste it on her tongue, feel it in the heavy pumping of her heart. Because of his lies, these were her useless choices. The only miserable choices her stubborn heart and pride would allow her to make.

Because of Mitch's selfishness and her own stupidity, she and Jake had been separated for so long—when they should have been together.

When they should have been in love.

Should have had the chance to share their lives with one another.

Jake stared down at her, the heat pouring off his golden skin beating against her in waves, penetrating her dented armor, digging beneath the surface. "And if I change your mind? If I get it through that thick little head of yours that I want more from you than forty-eight hours worth of fucking? That I want an entire lifetime of it? If I can do it, then I stay, don't I, Taylor?"

Her stubborn chin lifted, her eyes drilling into his, almost hating him too, for being so cruel as to tempt her with the one thing she wanted above all others. Only he didn't look cruel. He looked like a man hurting for the woman he loved, but she couldn't believe it. A woman who hadn't told him she loved him back. No...she wouldn't believe it! No matter how friggin' convincing he looked. "Yes, but I have a condition."

The corner of his mouth kicked up and he lifted his hand to twist one puffy nipple between two work-roughened knuckles, pulling a sharp gasp from between her lips. His other hand thrust between her legs, thumb and forefinger pinching her clit, holding it with just the right amount of pressure till he could feel her heartbeat pumping against his fingers. They were deliberate actions, meant to show her that no matter how hard she might think of fighting him, her body already knew exactly who it belonged to. He owned it, and he was going to fuck it and tongue it and love it however and whenever he damn well pleased, no matter how many stipulations she tried to put on him.

His fingers moved the barest bit, pulling nipple and clit until she had to bite down on her lip to keep from moaning. He smiled, looking cocky and arrogant, and whispered, "What's your condition, sweetheart?"

"Um—"

Think...think! Oh yeah. "You can't—I mean, I don't want you telling me that...that you love me. You're not allowed to say anything like that again because we both know how ridiculous it is."

And if I have to listen to it I'm going to start believing it and I can't take that kind of chance.

"Fine." He didn't like it, but he'd live with it, because he had every intention of showing her how he felt every minute they spent together. He'd show her with his body and his mouth and his cock how much he loved her till he'd convinced every precious little cell from her head down to her toes.

Of course, he couldn't help but appreciate the irony of it all. For years he'd been fucking women who wanted more from him than the physical pleasure he was willing to share with them. And now that he had the one woman, the only woman, he'd ever wanted to give more to—the one he could give everything to, who already owned his heart—she didn't want it.

If God was a woman, she was up in heaven right now laughing her sweet little ass off at him.

He grabbed Taylor, tossing her back up on the bed so quickly she actually bounced. "If sex is all I can have from you, all that you want from me," he gritted through his teeth, following her down, moving over her, "then I'll take as much as I can get."

She lay beneath him, a look of wary caution falling over her fey features, but she wasn't telling him no. Jake nudged her knees apart, shoving her legs wide, knees bent, and looked down at her glistening pussy. His fingers moved through the pearly juice-soaked curls, over the naked, gleaming lips, playing with them. Her slit was quivering, gasping, leaking more of her sweet tasting cream, and he shook his head in awe, his mouth twisting in an odd expression that made her want to cringe and cover herself.

"What's wrong with me?"

Dark green, heavy-lidded eyes snapped to hers. "There's not a damn thing wrong with you. It's just that every time I look at you, the shock of it hits me again. I've never seen anything like you, Taylor. You're just so incredibly beautiful, it knocks the wind right outta me."

An embarrassed, sort of scoffing sound broke from her throat.

"I'm not bullshitting you, sweetheart. It's the truth, whether you choose to believe it or not. You're just so delicate and pretty and pink."

And it was true. He'd thought he'd seen it all, every kind of woman there was, every possible body type, from the overtly sexy to the shyly pretty, but he'd never seen anything like Taylor. She always looked so sweet, so virginal, it was nearly impossible to pull his eyes away. He laid his head on her thigh, ignoring her tense groan, and continued stroking her, petting her, for the moment just happy to be touching something so precious. And letting her know exactly who owned it. The anger was still burning in his blood, waiting to be set free, but for now it was enough just to have her like this, completely open and at his mercy, waiting for whatever it was he wanted to do to her.

One blunt, work-roughened finger stroked down the center of the tender flesh, circling the tiny slit of her vulva, and he nearly died when more pearly drops of cream spilled from the swollen mouth. He watched as he worked his big finger up into the constricting tightness, shuddering at the exquisite feel of her squeezing around him, slick muscles clenching him in hot wetness, and as he pulled it back out, his finger glistened with juice.

It was too much to resist. He leaned those few inches forward to lap her lightly with his tongue, teasing her with the tip. She felt him, he tasted her, and her hips rocked forward as he shoved his face into her again, his tongue penetrating that tiny opening, driving inside, and she came right into his mouth, pouring down his throat.

Jake growled into her, his throat working as he ate at her, trying to get deeper, and she clutched at his hair, pressing up against him, shameless with need as she pumped her pussy against his wet face.

And then suddenly he was rising over her again, his tongue, wet with her cream, plunging into her mouth as he grasped her hips, lifted her, and slammed his cock into her with a brutal, angry force. She cried out, but he was already pulling back, then ramming deeper. "Hell," he grunted, "I just want to stay inside of you forever, filling you full of me over and over and over again. You make me crazy with it, Taylor. Make me feel like a fucking animal!"

"Good!" she shouted, feeling the wild woman inside clawing to be set free. "Great. Be an animal, Jake. You aren't scaring me. I like you like this!"

One big hand twisted into the long mass of her hair, holding her still as he loomed over her, dark green eyes searching brown, seeking the truth. When he saw what he wanted, the same need staring straight back at him, dark and hungry, anger-tinged like a red glowing beast, he took her at her word and gave her exactly what she wanted.

With shocking speed, he pulled out of her and flipped her to her stomach, driving into her from behind before she'd even drawn her next breath. His fingers took a firm, almost bruising hold on her hips and he jerked her back against him until she'd taken him all the way to the root. He'd never, in all his life, been so far inside of a woman, never been pushed so deep, never been held so tight. And he wasn't surprised that he'd never found this kind of connection with a woman before now, because no other woman had ever held both his heart and his body.

They were Taylor's, if she'd only take them.

He pulled out and forced his way back in until her grasping muscles had swallowed him whole, surrounding him with warm, wet, intoxicating heat. The shocking perfection of being joined with her flooded through him all over again—even stronger this time—and he folded himself over her like an animal mounting its mate.

Then he rocked into her, pushing even further, and nipped at her sensitive lobe, his wicked tongue teasing into her ear. "Just think about it, Taylor. This is me and you. Before today I was dreaming about you every night, waking up hard for you every morning, thinking about you every minute of every day, and now I'm cramming your beautiful cunt full of cock and you're squeezing me like a fucking fist."

"I know," she moaned. "I know. I never thought this would happen." Another inch went in, pulling her pussy open, stretching skin that had never been penetrated so deep and so full, and never from this angle. The pleasure spilled through her in a rush, and she clenched tighter, pulling a ragged groan from his lips.

God, she felt like a virgin and it nearly killed him. "Tell me you've thought about this, Taylor. Tell me you've thought about what it'd be like having my cock inside of you all these years, breaking you open, making you mine."

She smiled through her tears, wiping them away on the pillow. "Too many times to count."

Beneath him she tightened—shivered. He began to move slowly, using nudging thrusts that worked his thick, ridged cock in and out of her in maddening degrees, creating a deliciously teasing friction. He drove her crazy for as long as he could, waiting until she was jerking back against him on her own, her body begging for more, and only then did he give her what she needed. Only then did he begin fucking her, taking her, ramming into her so that every grinding, forceful thrust of his cock could be savored and enjoyed by her insatiable cunt.

She wriggled her hips in a way he thought would drive him right out of his mind. Every hard muscle on his body was flexed tight, working him in and out of her, and he was actually afraid to turn his head and look at their reflection in the dresser mirror. He was pumping and sweating, his balls slamming against her clit, every facet of his being focused on plowing as deep into her as he could get.

She arched her back higher and he drove straight into that sweet hot spot deep inside of her that had been made just for him. The feelings broke over them in a writhing mass of flesh and need, showering them with sensation.

Taylor screamed, pushed right into another heart stopping orgasm, and Jake was right there with her, grinding his jaw down hard to keep from shouting the whole entire building awake. She clenched and squeezed around him, while he poured himself into her until it felt like his cock had turned itself inside out. They gasped and panted, wondering how anything that felt so much like death could feel so fucking good.

Finally all they could do was tumble atop the wrecked bedding like the survivors of a brutal shipwreck, struggling for life. Jake knew he must be too heavy, crushing her into the mattress, but he couldn't find the strength to move.

An eternity later she shifted, crawling over him as he fell to his back in utter exhaustion. She nuzzled up on his wide chest like a sleepy kitten, fitting as if she'd slept there forever, and Jake wrapped his arms around her, holding her close to the heavy thudding of his heart. The shadows of the moon fell, as did their eyes, and in their dreams they clung to one another, fearing they'd be torn apart again too soon—before they'd found the answer.

The last thought he had as he drifted away was a vow to do everything in his power to convince her, to win her trust and her love, even if it killed him.

Because there was no way in hell he wanted to go on living without her.

Chapter 11

In the early hours of dawn, Taylor woke to the teasing touch of Jake's lips sipping from her nipple, his fingers playing softly through her folds, bringing her to a slow, gentle burn that felt like dreaming.

She moaned in wonder, feeling her body go wet and warm, and he growled in response. "Can you take me again?" His deep voice was gritty both from sleep and the ache of desire.

Taylor stretched beneath him, arching into the touch of his lips and body and hands. "Even if I couldn't, I still would."

"I'd never hurt you," he whispered, and they both knew he meant more than just the physical pain of going another round.

The first rays of light struck through the curtains, not bright, but soft and shadowy, as if sneaking into a forbidden place. Against her lips, he said, "It's morning," at the same time the tip of his cock nudged between her moist folds, finding her sopping and hot and more than ready for him. He pressed within, working himself against the tight wetness of her body, and she moaned, "No."

Oh, God. His heart stopped, clenched tight with dread, thinking she'd end their bargain now and send him away, but then she whispered, "No, it's not morning yet. It's still our first night, Jake. I don't want our time to go by so quickly."

No, damn it. He wanted to rage and shout, knowing there was more here, more that needed to be said, but unable to think it through with her cunt drawing him in, her sweet tits pressed hard against his chest, her back arching her up into him. Jake grasped her slim hips with all ten fingers to hold her in place and plowed deep inside—forcing his way past her resistance with a powerful thrust that sent him surging in. Before she could find herself in it, he pulled out and drove into her again, taking her hard enough to hurt if she wasn't so wet and ready for him.

"Oh, God," she groaned. "I can't—it's too—oh, God."

Yeah, he thought. Fuck yeah. And he couldn't stop. He felt desperate with the need to make her feel it, to make her understand what he was trying to show her. This was his. All of it. All of her. He owned it. Her gorgeous body and sweet mouth, her laughter and tears and this beautiful pussy that sucked him tighter and wetter than any fist or mouth ever could, as if it really had been made just for him.

There was a spirituality to fucking Taylor that'd been missing with every other woman he'd ever had and he had to make her understand. He was driving his point home with the thick ramming of his body into hers, filling her up with it, saturating her as she broke and clenched and came in a pulsing rush around him, gripping his cock like a velvet lined little clamp.

They shuddered and moaned and fell asleep still glued together, and when she next opened her eyes, he was pressing into her again. The sun was shining bright behind the curtains, and she knew it was sometime late in the morning already. And there was Jake, staring down at her with all the love in the world shining in his dark green eyes, shifting, moving over her, his big, beautiful body crammed between her thighs, his cock plowing into her with each slow, claiming thrust.

He smiled down at her, pressing a chaste kiss to her lips, the innocent action so at odds with the way his cock was mercilessly laying claim to her sleep soft cunt. "Good morning, gorgeous" he rasped, his deep voice still scratchy from sleep, and with the dark growth of stubble on his cheeks he looked like a dark, dangerous pirate claiming his bounty.

She had a sudden flashback to a time when they'd still been in school. It'd been the night of a high school football game, and even though Mitch had insisted she go to watch him catch the winning touchdown, she'd gone to see Jake throw it. She'd gone to watch him and dream. He'd played beautifully, an amazing physical machine of strength, talent, and intelligence, and she'd ached at the sight of his big, beautiful body wrapped up tight in that delicious uniform that showed off every amazing detail.

They'd beaten the hell out of the visiting team, and afterwards there'd been a ceremony naming Jake MVP of the season. The mayor had been there to present the plaque, the crowd roaring cheers and congratulations, and it'd been the strangest thing, but she could've sworn Jake's dark green eyes had been on her the entire time. She'd been standing at the sidelines, lost in her oversized coat, trying to protect herself from the bitter cold of the wind and rain, but those eyes had searched her out, locked with her own, and they'd stayed there, hot and hungry and full of fire, until Mitch had showed up at her side and caught her up in his arms.

It'd been one of the oddest, most exciting moments of her life because for those brief, heart-stopping minutes, it was as if the rest of the world had ceased to exist and there was no one but the two of them. Two strangers, for all the time they'd ever spent with one another, and yet, the smoldering look in his eyes had been anything but distant. It had been deliciously intimate, almost like a physical touch, as if he'd stroked her naked skin beneath the layers of wool and cotton, and she'd gone home that night and touched herself for the first time.

She'd lain in her lonely bed, beneath the cold sheets, and put her fingers between the folds of her pussy, imagining they were Jake's. She'd writhed and moaned and begun to sweat, but had been unable to reach the release that had remained stubbornly out of her reach. Finally she'd just given up, screaming a roar of frustration into her pillow, and then dreamed of him throughout the long, fitful night, her body aching and hungry, throbbing, needing him like she'd never needed anything before.

And it'd remained aching and hungry and needy ever since—until last night.

And now she was here, pressed beneath his body, taken and penetrated and packed full to the point of bursting. My God, she loved the physical intimacy of it almost as much as she loved him. There was a vague, sleep-dazed memory of having done this in the early hours of the morning too, when the sun was only just beginning to rise, and she wondered with a small smile how the man could be so insatiable.

"It's you," he groaned against her soft lips, as if reading her mind. "I can't stop wanting you, Taylor. You're like a drug in my system. All I have to do is look at you or smell your wicked little scent or hell, just think about you, and I'm hard and aching to fuck."

Pushing up on his arms, he straightened them with his palms planted flat at her shoulders. His eyes locked on to the place where they joined, his cock stretching that tiny hole so friggin' wide, and his jaw tightened when he saw how brutal he looked pushing into her fragile, over-stretched flesh.

He pushed harder, and her voice broke as she cried, "Me too, Jake." Her body was on fire, liquid and scalding and aching, hungry for every long, thick inch as he worked himself in and out of her. "Me too."

He shifted above her, and she wanted to moan from the delicious press of his hard body against her own, but then he was doing something to her hips, twisting her, and suddenly she was on her side, one leg pushed up against her body, while Jake plowed himself inside of her, cramming even deeper at this strange angle. The head of his cock was rubbing against some wonderfully untouched spot, stroking it with increasing pressure, ramming into it, and suddenly she was gasping and crying and coming all over his cock, drenching him in cream.

"You like this, don't you, sweetheart?"

She shuddered beneath him, her face dark red, cries choppy and raw in answer, and he fucked her harder, ramming her full of him till he thought he must be slamming against the back of her throat. Her cunt was gripping and pulling, soaking him in hot, slippery heat, and he growled low in his throat as his orgasm pounded its way out of him. He pressed as deep as he could, holding himself there, loving the thought of filling her womb with his seed, praying that someday he'd be right here, with no hormonal barriers between them, and he'd be filling her up just like this and they'd make a baby together. A beautiful, wonderful baby that was just like its mother.

The first of many.

The beginnings of a family.

The beginnings of his life.

"Keep holding me while I sleep?" he asked huskily, his voice rough from physical exhaustion when he finally collapsed against her.

She smiled against the top of his silky head. "Of course."

He raised his head to look into her eyes, watching her from beneath the long, thick fringe of his lashes. She smiled again, thinking of him as a beautiful little boy and how he must've hated having such pretty eyelashes.

He leaned up to place a soft, sweet kiss against her smile. "Be here when I wake up so I can fuck you again?"

The smile slowly fell away, knowing he was afraid she was going to run out on him. "We have a deal, Jake. I'll be here."

"We have a hell of a lot more than a deal, Taylor." He placed a warm, lingering kiss to her heart, and fell asleep with his face planted there, buried between her sweet breasts.

He breathed deep and even, blanketing her in his heat and scent, her sex-flushed body replete with drowsy satisfaction. She stroked his hair, drifting into dreams, wondering how she was ever going to survive another night like the last. Wondering how she'd ever survive a lifetime without the man in her arms. And hating herself for knowing she'd never be able to find the courage to try and keep him.

She couldn't live every day waiting for the axe to fall, wondering who was on every call, worrying where he was when he left the house or came home late, the way she had with Mitch. Who could go through life like that? She'd done it once already and it'd been a living hell. And with Jake it'd be even worse, because she loved him. His betrayal would be more than a blow to her pride, the way it'd been with Mitch. It would rip her heart out, crush her, break her, and she couldn't risk it. There was so little left of her as it was.

God, this was so friggin' scary, and it seemed to Taylor that her fears only compounded the more time she spent with him. Fears about his feelings, and fears about her own. About what this was all leading to and how it would all end.

But most of all, she was terrified by the idea that she was dangerously starting to believe him.

Chapter 12

The morning was a lazy, sensual interlude meant to be enjoyed by lovers. They spent the time lying in bed, their bodies wrapped around one another, snuggling together as the sun climbed high into the sky and the rain drummed slowly against the windows. Only when their stomachs demanded refueling after all the endless hours of physical exertion did they abandon white cotton sheets for clothes, deciding to catch some fresh air and head out for a drive.

They grabbed coffee and pastries at a corner coffee shop, then drove around the prospering town of Pressmore, talking about which of Jake's old school buddies was doing what now and with whom. Taylor was surprised by how well they adjusted to the intimacy of going from strangers to lovers to friends, amazed to find herself so comfortable in his presence, when always before he'd made her so nervous she'd felt sick with it.

Of course, those churning butterflies and damp palms were still there, and that shortness of breath every time she found herself caught directly in that knowing green stare, but there was a newfound comfort in the knowledge that she affected him the same way. And it didn't take a leap of faith to believe it. Now she recognized the signs. The way the lines at the corners of his mouth went tense or his hands flexed, or the way he'd rub his hand across the back of his neck, his dark cheekbones tinged with faint color—

they were all clues that Jake was feeling the effect of her nearness as well.

And knowing he wanted her as badly as she wanted him lent a degree of easiness to their just being together, sharing stories and laughter and time that she'd never dreamed she'd find with another human being. The fact that it was Jake, the last person in the world she'd ever expected to feel "herself" with, only made it that much more meaningful.

They'd just decided on hitting Angelo's later for dinner, their metabolisms in overdrive after the hedonistic hours spent in bed, when Jake headed down an old road on the outskirts of town that weaved back toward Westin. They drove through the falling leaves of thick, overhanging trees, her heart skipping in a special way when he reached across the leather console to grab her hand, twining her slender fingers with his own larger ones. It was almost funny, the disparity in their sizes — and yet, they were a perfect fit.

As they neared the end of the old road, it merged into a rocky dirt track that finally sloped off at the edge of a hill overlooking a bubbling, picturesque creek, and in the near distance, several old, dilapidated apartment structures that had long ago ceased to be inhabited and were now slowly rotting into the ground.

Taylor's breath caught in her lungs, her hand shaking in Jake's sturdy grasp as she looked out over the odd beauty of the tableau below. It was a view she'd never seen before, at least from this angle, and she wondered how Jake had known to come here.

She looked at him, her eyes huge in her small face, and he answered her unspoken question. "I used to drive up here and watch you paint by the creek."

Her bottom lip trembled, and she pulled it between her teeth to stop the telling action. "I—I never knew, Jake." She looked back out over the scene. She looked out at what once had been the place she called home. "How come I never heard you?"

He laughed softly. "That creek runs pretty noisy, and you always seemed to be off in your own little world anyway. I probably coulda bulldozed down the hill and you'd have never noticed."

She shook her head in awed disbelief. "Why'd you do it?"

She sensed more than saw him shrug beside her. "Just to be close to you. You made me feel—hell, I don't know how to explain it. It just gave me this strange feeling of peace to be near you. I'd drive up here and watch you paint and everything just felt—right somehow. Better."

She dipped her chin, smiling a shy, beautiful smile, her cheeks going red with color, and then looked off into the distance to the apartments where she and her mother had lived and he followed her gaze. He'd hated that she'd had to live there, surrounded by drunks and drug addicts, people who her sorry-ass mother had fit right in with.

"God," she whispered, "I hated that place, with all the noise and fights and people."

"Your mother was a royal bitch."

She was startled by the unexpected outburst. "Um, yeah," she replied awkwardly, wondering just how much Jake knew of her childhood.

He shifted restlessly in his seat, muscles bulging and releasing, the inside of the cab going hot and thick with tension. "I saw you that day when she dropped you off in front of the school. You'd called Mitch to tell him not to pick you up, so I was worried and waited out in my truck for you to show up. When I saw you get out, you had blood running down your chin from your lip and your cheek was bruised."

His hands fisted in his lap, his knuckles white. "I had to fight to keep from getting out and smacking her pathetic ass into the ground. I've never hit a woman in my entire life, Taylor, but I wanted to hit her so badly I could taste it."

She cringed with the memory, hating that Jake had seen her like that. Hating the way her life had been. "I remember the day," was all she could think to say, not wanting to burden him with stories from her less than stellar upbringing.

He blew out a heavy breath, resting his head back on the seat. "Yeah, well, the only thing that kept me from reporting her to the cops was that Mitch said the school officials had already filed complaints against her."

She shrugged her shoulders. "Child Services looked into it for awhile, but she was a real charmer when she wanted to be."

Yeah, there weren't many happy memories for her here, but then, it hadn't exactly been an ideal time in her life. Not only had she had to deal with all her mother's problems, but school had been difficult, not from a grade standpoint, but a social one. It wasn't so much that she'd been excluded—she'd just sort of lived in her own world. When most teenage girls were poring over Seventeen and sneaking their mom's Cosmos, Taylor had been reading Catcher in the Rye for the fortieth time or studying whatever art books she could get her hands on. She'd never been a part of their world, but she'd wanted desperately to be a part of Jake's.

God, how many times had she sat on the banks of that stream and sketched in her journals, dreaming of him? Agonizing over why she was so invisible to him. Trying to figure out why he seemed to hate her with such venom when she'd never done anything to him. And now that she knew the truth, knew the true extent of Mitch's treachery, all those long, misspent hours seemed so miserably wasted and cruel. What would have happened to the course of her life if she'd ever found the courage to confront the man at her side when he'd been that beautiful green-eyed boy? What kind of woman would she be today?

Huh. She'd probably have a hell of a lot more backbone than the pitiful wreck she'd become. She'd probably be a woman who believed in herself enough to go after what she wanted and believe that she'd be able to hold it once she got her hands on it. She'd be the kind of woman that could've told Jake she loved him too, instead of throwing his incredible words back in his face, refusing to acknowledge them, pretending they'd never even been said.

God, she cried silently in frustration, screaming in her mind. Why couldn't she just turn to him and tell him what was in her heart? Tell him that he was the one, the only one, and he always would be. Tell him she wanted to be his wife and his partner and the mother of his children. Tell him she wanted to be the best lover he'd ever known. Tell him she wanted to be the only lover he ever had again. Tell him she wanted to spend the rest of her life with him and grow old with him and eventually die with him.

Trembling with the need of it all pouring through her body, she turned to him, and he must've been able to read it all on her face, see it in her eyes because he groaned and grabbed for her, dragging her across his lap. Then his wonderfully rugged hands were holding her head while his mouth devoured hers, capturing her tongue, eating at her as if he couldn't live without this tangle of lips and tongues and teeth.

"Taylor," he gasped into the moist cavern, his hands groping beneath the long hem of her fluttering gypsy dress, seeking her wet heat, digging beneath the edge of her panties until he was cupping her pussy, fingers seeking and playing along her swollen folds. "Please, baby. Let me have you, right here, right now."

"Yes," she hissed, already helping him by settling herself astride his lap, knees bent on the seat on either side of his hips, her fingers attacking the stubborn buttons of his fly while Jake tongued her nipples through the thin cotton of her dress. "Do you know what I would have done if I'd known you were up here, watching me, all those years ago?"

"What?" he growled, his entire body tensing, waiting, on the verge of explosion from the feel of her cool little hands on his fly and her huskily spoken words.

"I'd have come up here, asked you to let me in, and I'd have done this," she groaned, releasing the last button and wrapping her soft little fingers around the blistering hot skin of his cock. She stared into his eyes, loving the way they burned with so much need and emotion. "I'd have begged you to fuck me, Jake. I'd have taken your big, beautiful cock inside of me and rode you just like I always wanted to."

Sweat poured from his temples, into his wild eyes, over his flushed cheekbones. His throat worked, his body shaking beneath her. "I've never—" he grunted, so hot he could barely speak. "Never—never felt anything close to this. Close to you. I'd trade every fuck I've ever had just to have had one minute with you, Taylor. Thirty seconds. Five. Anything!"

His wicked hands ripped away the insubstantial barrier of her panties, clever fingers spreading her cream, making sure she was ready for him.

They both recognized the rightness of the moment, the beauty of it. The air inside the cab of the truck became humid with their panting breaths, the scent of their need filling the small space, flooding their senses.

"Fuck," he growled. "I feel like I'm eighteen again, desperate for that first time I'll get to sink inside of you, cramming you full of me, breaking you open. How in the hell do you do this to me, Taylor?"

"I don't know," she gasped, her pussy clenching in need as she watched him take his thick cock in his fist, guiding himself to her juicy slit.

Jake's eyes dropped down to the raunchy, beautiful sight of his hard cock prodding against her juice covered cunt. "I used to drive up here as often as I could," he grunted roughly, pushing further between her lips, angling his hips so he could watch the head of his cock begin to penetrate that sweet little slit, stretching her so wonderfully wide. "I used to watch you and dream of carrying you up here, of taking you in my truck just like this, and making love to you until neither one of us could remember our names."

He dragged his eyes away from the erotic sight, grasping her hips as he rammed up into her, burying himself all the way to his balls, and looked straight into her vague, passion-glazed eyes. "Not fucking," he growled, "but making love, Taylor. Do you understand me?"

"Yes," she cried out, wondering what kind of miracle made it possible for her to begin to move so sinuously above him, on him, riding his cock as if she'd done it a thousand times before, and knowing she was driving him to a wild, wonderful edge.

It was like some inherent, seductive knowledge buried deep in her psyche that Jake had unleashed; a primitive instinct to drive him outta his mind with the lithe press of her hips and the pull and clench of her gushing pussy. The effect she saw on his hard, beautiful face filled her with an intoxicating power. It pulsed through her blood, quickening her pulse, making her drunk on pleasure.

His cock was in fucking ecstasy, soaked in her cream, and his thumb snaked between them, swiping her clit, collecting some to taste. Jake brought his wet thumb to his mouth, his tongue flicking for a quick swipe, making sure to save enough for her. She moaned over his feral growl of pleasure, and then he rubbed his thumb across her bottom lip, leaving a glistening smear of her cream behind.

With one hand fisted into her hair, Jake pulled her face to his until their breaths were mingling, the tips of their noses nearly touching. "I told you before, Taylor, this is my cunt now." His hips thrust hard, plowing his big cock up tighter into her, making them both shake with the hunger for more. "I've claimed it—and I'll kill any bastard who ever tries to take it away from me again!"

She moaned, and his mouth swallowed the sound, covering hers. His tongue licked eagerly at her lip, then filled her mouth, moving in perfect rhythm with the thrust of his cock so deep inside of her.

And when he had to come up for air, their lungs burning, bodies on fire, he gave her one of the most shocking admissions of all. "Mitch told me how you hated living down there," he grunted, his voice choppy from the rhythm of their bodies moving together, the sexy little way she was riding his cock, her cunt a rippling sheath of grasping muscles and liquid heat nearly driving him outta his mind. "Not that I couldn't see it on my own, but he told me how you dreamed of designing your own house someday. Something that was yours. Something special."

She was locked into his eyes, wondering what he was trying to tell her, almost afraid to know the answer. She was too much under his spell as it was.

"It's because of you, Taylor." His eyes were blazing now, his body hot and hard and shuddering, and she knew he was about to come. "The reason I learned to build houses—it's because of you!" His hands found the sides of her face, pulling her mouth back to his, their breaths merging as completely as their sexes. "I did it so I could build you your dream house someday, Taylor. So I could come back and give you one of the things you'd always wanted for your very own."

She cried out as the meaning of his words roared through her, drenching her with love, and he swallowed the sweet sound down his throat just as they fell into that heart stopping little death and came against one another in a torrent of passion and love and need. Her arms wrapped around his head, holding him tight, while he held her hips, grinding her pelvis against his own, eating at her mouth as she shuddered and gasped and moaned.

The earth-shattering sensations were slow to fade, and he soothed her back to reality, stroking the silky skin of her back beneath her dress, smiling as she nuzzled up against his chest and fell into a trusting slumber. Jake savored the feel of her in his arms, the tender way her cheek snuggled against his heart with the innocence of a child. His arms wound round her tighter, his hands trembling from the force of emotion flooding through him, the fear that by this time tomorrow she might no longer be a part of his life burning in his gut like a sickness.

Christ, he couldn't lose her. Not again. Not now. Not ever.

"Rest now, sweetheart," he whispered into her hair as the wind howled and another slow rain began to fall, marveling at the fact that he was holding her in his arms, his softening cock still held tight within her body. "'Cause when we get back, you're going to need it."

One hungry thought led to another, and a wicked smile was just breaking across his face as her eyes blinked lazily up at him a quarter of an hour later.

"What?" she groaned warily, but her lips were twitching, looking forward to whatever it was he was scheming in that wicked mind of his.

He pressed a kiss to her lips. "Let's go for a ride."

"Where to?" she asked casually, trying to be cool about the fact that she was sliding off his wonderfully thick cock with their cum running down the insides of her thighs and her panties were somewhere in shreds. Somehow she didn't think this was one of those situations covered in young ladies' etiquette books. In fact, she was pretty bloody sure of it.

His smile kicked up at the corner, feral and hungry and wicked.

He was so bad, she thought dreamily as he handed her what was left of her underwear, his look clearly telling her he was looking forward to ripping the next pair off her as well. The kind of bad that a girl could never resist, and if she was smart, never even wanted to.

"I'm gonna surprise you," he drawled with a wink.

Taylor crawled back over to her seat, securing her own seat belt as he twisted the key in the ignition. He laughed huskily under his breath, his mind obviously already on wherever they were going, and it was fun just to see the excitement pumping through his system. He looked like a boy of eighteen again, all giddy with wicked delight.

More mind shattering fucking anyone?

Yeah, she thought, feeling her own heart begin to pound in anticipation. Why not? Why the hell not?

Chapter 13

"No."

Just that one word, emphatic and absolute. And then, "Not a chance in hell."

"Ah, come on, Taylor. Take a walk on the wild side."

She laughed under her breath. "Jesus, Jake, this is my wild side." Her finger pointed toward the dark storefront, where the sign on top elegantly scripted the name The Honey Pot. "This place is way, way past whatever wildness I have in me, big guy."

His eyes twinkled mischievously. "Yeah? When were you in there?"

Her lips pressed together, fighting back a smile. "I've never been in there, you dolt."

He winked at her. "Then how do you know what they have in there?"

"My imagination works just fine, thanks."

He reached over her, pulling his wallet out of the glove compartment. "All right, I guess I'll just have to go in there by my lonesome then."

Taylor laughed beside him, shaking her head at his outrageousness. "You're just gonna walk all by yourself into a sex shop and it's not even going to bother you, is it?"

"Naw," he drawled, leaning over to give her a warm, wet, lingering kiss. "I want what's in there too bad to worry about what other people think. Besides, the only person I give a shit about is you, and you already think I'm a pervert."

He opened his door to climb out, and she couldn't help but eye the entrance with a jealous curiosity, wishing she was bold enough to just get out and do it. But the sidewalks were far from empty and she knew she'd never see it through. Jake gave her a warm, sexy smile, reading her thoughts as easily as his own. "How about I check it out this first time, and next time you can go in with me if you want?"

"Deal," she said quickly, before she could change her mind.

"One of several," he murmured, his eyes telling her he was talking about the other deal they had going, and she was suddenly a little worried about what he'd find in there. Whatever it was, she had to do it, according to their agreement, and that thought was as disturbing as it was exciting. The only thing that kept her from opening her door and getting the hell out of there was the fact that she trusted Jake implicitly.

Well, she trusted him with her body. Her heart was another matter altogether.

She watched him disappear into the modest looking storefront, and she couldn't help but wonder at what he'd find inside. But since the front windows were tinted and she couldn't see what was happening in there anyway, she took the opportunity to brush the tangles out of her hair and then flipped down the passenger's side visor, hoping for a mirror to retouch her lip gloss.

The mirror was there, but all thoughts of make-up slipped from her mind as she stared into the reflective surface.

Her eyes opened wide, surprised to find that the overtly sexual, decadent reflection staring back at her was her own. She looked wild and wanton, like some fairy creature stolen from a primeval forest. For the first time in her entire life, she looked like one of the otherworldly beings she painted instead of the dowdy, demure painter who created them.

For the first time ever, she looked like a satisfied woman.

A woman who had been well-handled and fucked, wonderfully debauched, taken hard and long and rough in the steamy cab of Jake Farrell's truck.

A woman who had been well and thoroughly loved.

The wild woman inside of her wanted to curve her lips in a victorious smile, stretch her glowing, lithe little body in a sinuous, sensuous arc against the seat, and bring the beautiful male animal inside that sex shop to his knees. She wanted to bathe in the hot, blazing flame of lust she knew would be smoldering in his green eyes. Wanted to gorge herself on it until it'd stretched her skin and she had to break away from the world or burst at the seams.

The wild woman wanted to be inside that shop with her man.

And suddenly Taylor realized she wanted the exact same thing. She was done hiding out in the truck like the "old" Taylor, willing to sit back and watch as life passed her by, while her man went to buy sex toys by himself.

Screw this.

She was woman enough to go wherever she damn well pleased. Even if it was a sex shop!

Screw being shy. Screw letting her man just walk away.

Fired with determination, her heart pounding in excitement, Taylor latched onto the door handle, ready to fling it open, when she caught sight of him.

She caught sight of Mitch.

Holy shit. He was standing on the opposite side of the street, wearing his sheriff's uniform and aviator sunglasses, making it impossible to see his ice blue eyes behind the mirrored lenses. Still, his rigid posture and the hard set of his mouth told her exactly what he was thinking.

He'd seen who she was with and for some bizarre ass reason, he didn't like it. All the lies he'd told came flooding back to her. All the pain caused by hearing him tell her how much Jake disliked her, the cruel things he'd made up, and for a split second she grabbed the door handle tighter, ready to jump out and slap his cocky face for all the malicious heartache he'd caused.

He hadn't wanted her, but for some unfathomable reason, he hadn't wanted Jake to have her either. And now it was too late for any of them because she no longer trusted herself. All the years of pain and humiliation pressed down on her and it was almost like suffocating, feeling her throat close up, choking on regret.

She closed her eyes, feeling caught between her past and her future. On one side of the street was Mitch, who'd systematically tried to dismantle her feelings of confidence and self-worth, while on the other side, buying God only knew what in the little upscale sex shop, was the only man who'd ever made her feel like a beautiful, desirable woman. The only man she'd ever loved. And because of the one, she was too afraid to take a chance on the other. Her heart clenched, already feeling the pain of when Jake would be gone. An empty ache that would grow over the years, worse now that she knew how incredible it felt to have him buried deep inside of her, a part of her, held against her heart.

This was so fucking unfair, and her hands shook in her lap as the rage poured up from inside of her. Rage at Mitch for marrying her when he didn't want her. Rage at herself for believing his lies. For marrying him when she didn't love him. For never going after Jake when they were young and she still believed in happily ever afters and they might have had a chance.

The sound of the driver's side door unlocking jolted her eyes open, and Mitch was gone. The sidewalk was empty. Her hands unclenched, smoothing over her thighs, and she forced a smile as she turned back to Jake. He climbed into the big truck, her breath catching like it always did with her first look at him, and hot tears were suddenly burning behind her eyes, threatening to spill over.

She held them back with the full force of her will, afraid that once they slipped free, she'd never be able to stop them. Jake twisted to place a blue paper bag on the backseat and then turned back to her, his eyes seeing past her false smile, straight into her soul.

He reached out, smoothing a strand of hair from her temple and tucking it behind her ear. "What happened, honey? You okay?"

She nodded her head, praying her voice wouldn't tremble. "I'm fine, but do—do you think we could just grab some food and eat back at the hotel? I don't really feel much like going out anymore."

His green eyes showed his concern, and her heart twisted harder. Oh yeah, she definitely hated herself for not trusting this man with her heart. He'd offered her love and she'd rejected it. But no matter what was in that mysterious blue bag, she was going to trust him with her body. She owed him that much, after everything he'd admitted to her, even if she couldn't really believe all of it. Hell, she owed him everything.

"Whatever you want, Taylor. You name it, honey, and it's yours." He stroked the outline of her lips with one blunt fingertip, his eyes going dark and hungry with more than just sexual need. "Haven't you figured that out by now?"

She took a slow, deep breath, unwilling to admit anything of the sort. Instead, she whispered, "Thanks, Jake," and leaned over to give him a quick, chaste kiss on his cheek.

For a split second his mouth twisted with regret, as if he knew what was going through her head, and then he started the engine, pulling into the gentle flow of early evening traffic. Taylor laid her head back against the headrest, trying to ignore the truth she'd heard in his words and the way they knifed into her heart, determined to ignore the little voice inside her head telling her she was a fool and an idiot. Then Jake's big hand reached into her lap, grabbing hold of her own, engulfing her with his size, yet holding her hand so gently, and she turned to look out her window into the safety of the night as those stupid tears began to fall.

Chapter 14

Something had happened, ruining the easy mood of the afternoon, and Jake was damned if he knew what it was. Taylor had cried all the way to the fast food joint, but by the time he'd asked what she wanted to eat, she'd gotten herself back under control and he pretended he hadn't noticed she'd had hot tears spilling over her cheeks.

But their time was running out and he was done pretending. "Taylor, we need to talk."

"No."

He hated the cold, distant look falling over her face, like she was closing up on him, and a fresh surge of anger burned through him, powered by frustration and fear. She was shutting him out, not even giving him a chance, and he felt as if he were already losing her. His time was nearly gone, and the anger in his blood only made him that much more determined to break through to her in the only way she seemed to understand. If she wouldn't listen to his heart, then she was sure as hell going to get the message from his body.

"You don't want to talk? Fine," he muttered, propping himself up on the bed pillows, watching her rummage nervously through her suitcase, searching for God only knew what. "Take off the dress."

She snorted, almost making him smile, but it was strained because he was nearing his limit. "Come on, Taylor. You agreed to fuck me for forty-eight hours and we're only halfway down. And I've been thinking about your sexy little body underneath all that soft cotton all damn day. Now drop the dress like I told you to do and let me see it."

Her head shook in disbelief. "You like scrawny girls suddenly, Jake? Somehow I don't think so. And we've already had sex today, twice this morning and then in your truck. There's nothing under here you haven't already seen."

"This morning doesn't count because we hadn't even gotten dressed yet, and you weren't naked in the truck. I got to feel it, but I didn't get to see it. And for your information," he rumbled, "I like you!"

He was careful not to use the wrong "L" word and send her running. "I like your soft tits, and that heart shaped ass, and everything else from the top of your pretty little head down to those sexy little toes. And I especially like that sweet, fist-tight little cunt between your legs. I like the way it looks, the way it smells, the way it tastes and the way it feels wrapped around my cock. Now take off the dress, Taylor, so I can see you before I come over there and rip the thing to shreds!"

"I never knew you could be such a bully," she muttered, but he could see the need burning in those sable-colored eyes, slowly overtaking the uncertainty. By the time he'd reacquainted himself with every delicious inch of her, she'd never have any doubt how she affected him. And he'd happily fuck her into conviction every single day and night for the rest of his life, if she'd only give him the chance to prove himself.

She turned around, giving him her back, making him smile at her shyness. Making him look forward to ridding her of her stupid hang-ups. Who in the hell would want to grind against another woman when they could have Taylor, with her sexy as hell looks and soft, womanly body? She may not be stacked or built like a swimsuit model, but she was just what he wanted. He didn't know why she was so insecure about her perfect little curves, but he was looking forward to showing her in dirty, explicit detail just how much he loved them.

The dress fell to the floor in a soundless heap, and he had to swallow over the lump of lust in his throat to see the naked line of her spine and that rosy ass barely covered in the sheer pair of nude panties she'd put on the minute they made it back to the room.

"Turn around," he growled, sounding like a fucking animal. Any second now and he was gonna be all over her.

She turned slowly, her arms crossed over her breasts, the soft, satiny mounds pressed up tight against her chest, and he nearly swallowed his tongue. Her belly was smooth perfection, her slim hips just right for a man to sink his fingers into and fuck his way to heaven. His eyes went lower, and there it was, the prettiest little cunt he'd ever seen, the demure lips just visible through the sheer panties that let him see it all. He couldn't wait to spread her open again and look his fill. He wanted to take a fucking magnifying glass to her and study every delicious, precious inch of her pussy — to know it better than the only other man who'd ever been lucky enough to get anywhere near it.

He wanted — no, needed — had to claim it for his own. Shit, it was only fair, considering his cock had belonged to her for years now. A lifetime, if he was completely honest. "Move your arms."

She lowered them slowly, clasping them around her waist, which only pushed the sweet swell of her breasts higher. She had tiny, puffy pink nipples the same color as her lips and he loved them. Loved their texture and taste and the way they fit so delicately inside his mouth. "Now the panties. Walk to the end of the bed, take them off and hand them to me."

She shook her head.

"You made a deal to do everything I said, Taylor. You backing out already?"

She moved forward, her breasts gently swaying, and his cock nearly broke through his fly then and there. Then she bent over, pulled down the insubstantial panties and tossed them onto his outstretched hand. His fingers closed around the damp fabric, making a fist. "You're wet, Taylor, and I haven't even touched you yet. Climb up here. Right on the end of the bed there."

She started to sit down, and he growled, "No. I want you on your knees. Then spread your legs as wide as you can."

"Why?" she asked uneasily, eyeing the blue bag on the nightstand out of the corner of her eye.

He didn't even look her in the face, his eyes glued to her glistening pink folds. "'Cause I wanna see your cunt again and you're gonna show it to me. Right now."

She laughed softly, thinking they both must be crazy. "Yeah? And what are you going to show me?"

Jake rose to his knees on the mattress in front of her in one fluid movement, somehow oddly graceful for a man of his size. His smile taunted her as his fingers began ripping at the buttons of his fly. "If you wanna see my cock, sweetheart, all you have to do is ask. Anytime. Anywhere."

She stared in rampant need and excitement. "Yes, please," she whispered, making him groan and laugh and shudder with lust all at once. Then it was springing into the air between them, a good nine inches or more of thick, rock hard, throbbing empurpled flesh. God, she wanted to cry at the beauty of it. His balls were dark, heavy sacs beneath, the shaft thicker than her own wrist, and the head was like something from a...a...she didn't know what. It was broad and round, kind of heart-shaped, and there were already trickles of pre-cum streaming from the slit in its tip.

Without thinking, she reached out to touch it, but he grabbed her wrist, shaking his head, his eyes burning like two otherworldly fires of sex and pain and flesh. They were promising her things she'd never even imagined. "Don't touch me," he snarled. "Not yet, or I'll be buried deep before you know what hit you. And I wanna see it first. I wanna see that juicy little thing that belongs to no one but me now."

She started to move toward him, but he shook his head. "Lie down on your back with your head over the edge so you can watch me in the mirror. Then open your legs for me and put them out on either side of my body."

With her limbs shivering, shuddering, her breath coming in rapid pants of air, Taylor lay down just as he said. When she could see him in the mirror, his eyes caught hers and she began opening her thighs, praying she could see this little scenario through without giving him everything.

He watched as she forced them wider, moving slowly toward her down the bed, and she forced them wider still, till she was spread eagle and he was on all fours, his face no more than a foot away from the sweet juncture of her thighs.

He looked up at the mirror, his face a taut expression of the kind of hunger she thought could exist only in a woman's mind. She'd never thought she'd have a man look at her that way, and her pussy flooded even more, becoming embarrassingly wet, unbearably empty.

Jake looked down at the sight before him, stroking his tongue against the roof of his mouth in a restless gesture of hunger. It was even better than he'd imagined—better than he'd remembered—so rosy and small, just waiting for him to fuck her long and hard and deep. Her clit was already throbbing, her lips swollen and soft, completely bare, and her vulva was gasping for air like a little mouth, streaming juices, wet and pink like the inside of a flower.

Her sweet scent hit him hard, and a noise like none other he'd ever made climbed up the back of his throat. He hoped it didn't scare the hell out of her. But she only moaned in response, her hips lifting the barest fraction, offering that juice soaked little pussy up to his mouth.

"Tell me, Taylor. Did you enjoy being eaten out last night?"

Her breath stuttered and her voice trembled. "Um—"

"If you don't give me an answer, I'm gonna have to take it for a no."

"No," she moaned, trying to get the right words out. "I mean yes—yes, I loved it. You know I did."

He looked up at her from beneath his brows again. "What's it feel like when I put my tongue in you? When it pushes into that tiny opening and I eat you into my mouth?"

She shuddered beneath him, a fine sheen of sweat glistening over her pale skin. "Um—that's kind of a personal question, Jake."

He laughed a dark, dangerous sound. "And the fact I'm about to have my tongue shoved up your cunt isn't personal, honey? It doesn't get much more personal than that, so answer the damn question."

"Fine!" she gritted through her teeth, wondering where he was trying to push her with this. "It feels incredible, okay? Warm and wet and beautiful, but raunchy and rough too. There! Are you happy now?"

He looked back down at her. "Not yet, but I'm about to be."

She started to bring her legs together in a fit of temper, not really sure what she was mad about, but his big hands caught the inside surfaces of her thighs, pinning them down hard. "Don't even think about it."

"What about you, Jake? How many women have you gone down on? Hah, like this is something new for you. It's probably been hundreds, thousands! You've probably slept with every woman you've ever known! Probably shoved your tongue inside of more than you can even remember!"

"Yeah," he muttered, stroking a finger down the moist slit from her clit to her ass, "there's been more than a few." He spread her lips wide so he could see everything. "But I've never wanted anyone like this. I wish I could tell you there'd never been anyone else, almost as much as I wish you could tell me Mitch never saw you like this. Never fucked you. Never came screaming your name. But they didn't mean anything to me, Taylor. And if you think I'd ever want another woman now that I've had you, then you're outta your fucking mind!"

Before she could make a sharp comeback, he circled her vulva with that one rough fingertip and then shoved the whole thick digit up into her. Taylor saw stars swim before her eyes, her back arching off the bed as he drew the long finger out and then shoved in two, twisting them up into her, bringing a raw cry from her throat. "Oh—oh shit!"

"You like that?" he demanded roughly. "Yeah, me too. You're so tight, whenever I get inside of you, you just squeeze the cum right outta me."

She writhed beneath him, working herself on his fingers, and he loved it. Loved everything about her. "I need your taste again," he growled down at her, staring at his fingers penetrating the tiny little opening, watching with hungry desperation the way she creamed around the thick intrusion of his fingers, pearly and sweet. "Put your fingers down here and get them wet."

She moaned, but did as she was told, rubbing her fingers against the base of his own, coating them until they were slick and wet.

"Now put them in my mouth and let me taste you, sweetheart. It's been hours since I had your cream in my mouth, felt you coming down my throat."

She quivered in response, but followed his command. Jake sucked the clean juices from her small fingers with greedy satisfaction as they pressed past his lips, loving her flavor. She was hot and sweet and sexy as hell. "Fuck, you're so good," he grunted. "That's the sweetest little cunt I've ever tasted, Taylor. The only one I'll ever want—ever!"

Pushing her hips up against him, she rode his fingers as hard as she could, and then he was working a third up into her, shoving it in, and Taylor started screaming somewhere between the burning sting and blinding rush of pleasure from being so filled, so exposed.

She sounded in pain, but Jake knew enough about women to know it was a good kind. Still, she was so narrow and small, and he couldn't help but worry about all the fucking they'd been doing. "We need to get you stretched some more, okay, baby?" He moved over her, putting his mouth just over her left nipple, pleased to see it'd already hardened into a tight little bud. "I'm just gonna finger fuck you for awhile until you get ready for me again because once I get my cock in here, I'm gonna hammer the hell out of you with it."

"I am ready," she wailed, crying, on the verge of begging. "Oh God, now, Jake! Please! Anything, just—I need you."

He laughed, but it was a rough, ragged sound that had everything to do with pleasure and nothing to do with humor. "You're gonna do everything I tell you to, aren't you, sweetheart? Outside of the bedroom, we'll be perfect partners, equals, but in bed, you're gonna let me fuck you whenever and however I want. Aren't you, Taylor?"

"Yes," she cried, holding his eyes in the mirror, trying to convey with a look everything she was feeling. Then his head lowered and she felt the rough scrape of his tongue right across her nipple, watching it, holding his eyes, and she couldn't even breathe anymore. Sharp pleasure flooded through her, drenching his fingers and her thighs, and he really began working her with them, cramming his fingers out and back in, closing his mouth over the pretty mound of her breast and sucking hard enough to make her shout.

She was bucking beneath him, riding his hand, and he moved to the other breast, drawing it in, working his throat to take in as much as could, biting and licking and sucking until he heard her muttering, "Oh shit...oh shit...oh shit."

"You want more?" he asked around her nipple, digging his thumb into her clit, burying his fingers deep.

"Yes! God, yes — more!"

"Hmm, you're so close. How should I make you come this first time tonight? Do you know what I want to do to you?"

"Yeah," she gritted through her clenched teeth. "I think so."

He smiled against her breast, burying his face in the fragrant valley between them, ready to play with her for the rest of his life, knowing he'd never had a hotter woman in bed. Never had one so wet and tight and sweetly gorgeous, who made him want to come just from looking at her. Who could make him laugh and smile and make his heart stop just with a look from those big brown eyes.

Talk about scary fucking shit.

Or maybe it wasn't scary at all?

"If I tongue you," he said against her navel, moving lower, licking and biting along the way, "will you come down my throat and let me eat out all your sweet little juices again? Will you fill me up with them? Will you cream all over me, baby?"

He licked her hipbone, his fingers slipping free, stroking her lips, her vulva, then lower between the cheeks of her ass.

"Is that—is that what you want?"

"Oh, Taylor," he laughed, nuzzling her sexy little patch of hair with his nose, his cheek, breathing in huge lungfuls of her erotic scent. "I'm not gonna be a happy man till you let me go down on you five—six times a day at least. Say for the next forty or fifty years? That sound good to you?"

"Jake," she groaned.

"Yeah?" he smiled, nudging her clit with his nose, teasing them both. He caught it in his teeth and gave a gentle tug.

"Now, damn it!"

Fuck. He closed his eyes, took another deep breath, but it was too late, too much.

Suddenly his thumb was crammed up inside of her in a place she'd never imagined he'd touch and his tongue was eating its way deep into her pussy, his mouth ravenous in its claim, going at her with lips and tongue and teeth. His thumb wiggled and his tongue began plunging, withdrawing, fucking her just like he'd promised.

"Hell, you taste too good," he growled, biting at her lips, using his other hand to spread them open, licking and plunging inside, unable to get enough. It was a savage tongue-fuck, one meant to consume. "I've never tasted anything like you. You're fucking incredible, Taylor."

"I need more!" she cried, thrusting her hips forward, shoving her pussy in his face.

"Oh, you'll get more, sweetheart," he growled lovingly, flicking her clit with his sharp tongue. "As much as you can take, for the rest of your life."

He flicked her clit again, and she almost broke, but he pulled his mouth and tongue away, keeping the teeth-grinding orgasm just out of her reach. Then he was moving her around and lifting her up the bed, tossing her on the pillows, and his cock was driving inside. There was no gentle tease into penetration, no smooth entry. Just his thick erection cramming itself between her lips before she'd even settled, straight into her, and he immediately began taking her in a hard, delicious rhythm. Hard enough to wrench a sob-like cry with each impossibly deep, pounding thrust.

He filled her cunt up to the knife-edged point of pain, then hurtled her far beyond into the realm of searing, mindless sensation. Supporting his upper body on one muscled forearm by her head, he grasped her fingers in his free hand and lowered them to where they joined. Without breaking his plunging tempo, he directed her so that together they could feel the impossibly stretched, taut edge of her vulva as his body pounded into her.

"Feel what you do to me, Taylor. You're so tight and wet, I'm all but ready to explode just from being in you." He drew out of her, then plowed back in — deeper, harder, faster — and she made a noise that was part shock, part savage satisfaction. "But you do love to feel me move, don't you, baby? You love feeling me fuck this sweet little pussy. God, I can see the answer written all over your face."

"Don't...stop...Jake," she panted, not even caring that she was pleading. This was what she wanted. This mindless surrender of her body to the ruthless demands of his will—the grinding slide of his body into hers. This was what she needed to fill herself up on. "Please. Just. Don't. Stop."

"I won't," he promised, raking her mouth with a hungry, violent kiss. "I can't stop. I...can't...stop...fucking...you."

Not ever.

She half laughed, half groaned. "You have the dirtiest mouth I've ever heard, Jake Farrell."

A devilish gleam entered his eyes. "Mmm. I don't know?" He licked his lips, slowly, drawing out the seductive action. "When it's filled with your cream, I don't see how my mouth could be anything but sweet." Then he kissed her softly, rubbing his tongue along her lips, gently dipping inside to share her sugary taste. "See what I mean? I love the way your pussy tastes. Like it was made all special just for me."

"Oh, God." How could she still blush with embarrassment after everything they'd done together? Everything they were doing at that very moment!

Jake laughed knowingly, trailing kisses across her burning cheeks. "You love it when I talk dirty, Taylor." And you love me, he longed to say aloud, but kept the tempting words buried deep inside. Instead, he said in a low, seductive tone, "Now tell me what else you love. I want to hear you say it."

"Jake," she groaned, writhing beneath him. "I don't know how to talk like you."

Wanting to see more of her, he raised up on his arms, finding the sight of her naked, gleaming body moving in need, jolting with his deep strokes, the most erotic thing he'd ever seen. She drove him wild, no two ways about it, and he wanted to drive her just as crazy.

And now was the perfect time to do it.

Taylor whimpered in need as he pulled out of her, her body surging in panic at the loss of his hard, thick heat. "What—what are you doing?"

He smiled slow and sexy and self-assured, knowing he'd get exactly what he wanted in the end. Gripping his cock in his fist, he rubbed the wide head against her drenched sex, teasing the puffy slit, laughing when she lifted her hips, trying to take him back inside. "Not yet," he murmured, his green eyes promising everything she wanted and then some.

His smile turned wicked, and he said in a husky, lust-thickened voice, "I want to do something new with you, Taylor. Something I've never done with anyone else before." His green eyes shifted to the bag from The Honey Pot, his expression wry, yet smoldering with excitement. "Well, several things I've never done with anyone else."

Things? What kinds of things?

Before she could find her voice to ask, he'd reached over and pulled a long black satin cord out of the bag and was wrapping the silky binding around the fragile bones of her wrists, securing them together. Then he raised them above her head and tied the ends around one of the sturdy wooden slats of the headboard.

Holy shit! He'd tied her up!

Taylor stared at her bound wrists, tugging experimentally to find they didn't hurt, but were strongly secured, not giving an inch. "Um, Jake?"

"Yeah?" he drawled, his hand suddenly rummaging back in the bag and pulling out a very long, very thick Pyrex dildo.

Her eyes bugged and her heart stuttered. It was beautiful, in a strange, wicked way, made of swirled blue glass, the tip wide like the head of a cock. Jake held it before her, letting her get a closer look.

She tried to blink it into better focus, but her eyes were shocked wide, huge, watching it as if it were a poisonous snake about to strike. She wasn't afraid of it, but her emotions were a chaotic jumble, difficult to sort out.

Excitement.

Curiosity.

And an underlying nervousness that she was going to screw this up somehow. What in the hell did she know about dildos? And huge, blue glass ones at that.

"Um," she finally mumbled, after staring like a simpleton for what seemed like forever. "I, uh, didn't know guys liked to share."

Yeah, she was pretty sure it was a stupid thing to say, but then she didn't know if there was actually a smart thing to say at a time like this either. Pretty much all she wanted to do was keep staring—and maybe think about asking just what in the hell he planned on doing with that thing.

He shrugged his wide shoulders and smiled. "I'd never share you with another man, or hell, another woman for that matter. In fact, I'd fucking kill any bastard who even tried it, but I don't mind this little guy," and he winked at her, adding, "so long as you only use him when I'm around."

She couldn't help it; she laughed. "Jealous, are you?"

"Naw," he drawled, running the cool glass shaft between her quivering breasts. "I'm bigger than him anyway. But I saw something in a movie once when I was a horny, hormone raging teenager, and damn if I haven't fantasized about doing it with you ever since. You, Taylor. No one else. Ever."

"What—what was it?" she stammered, her breath sucking in on a sharp gasp as he trailed the huge phallus down her trembling stomach and pressed the cold tip against the warm lips of her cunt.

"I think I'll just show you instead," he rasped, swirling it just inside the rim of her vulva, watching it go wet with her cream. Her back arched, her heart pounding in need and unmistakable excitement. "If I didn't know better, honey, I'd say you're enjoying yourself." Then he let it slip lower, playing over the tight bud of her ass where his thumb had been, and she stopped breathing altogether.

"Jake," she croaked. "Jesus, what are you doing?"

He pulled his eyes away from the fascinating sight of watching blue Pyrex play against her skin to look into her eyes. "Trust me, Taylor."

It was as much a question as it was a statement. "Yes," she whispered, knowing that for some bizarre reason, considering he had her tied up and was about to do God only knew what to her with an intimidating glass cock, she did trust him—completely.

He smiled at her, laying the dildo on her butterfly-filled stomach to reach into the bag again. She held her breath in fascinated horror, exhaling a deep sigh of momentary relief when he withdrew a small bottle of what looked like oil. He popped it open and began to drizzle the warm, cinnamon sugary scent over her body, from her puffy nipples down to the dripping pink folds of her sex. When she was wet and running with rivulets of the amber liquid, he picked the dildo up again and poured the erotically scented oil over its wide tip until it gleamed. Then he set down the bottle and began warming the blue shaft of glass between his big palms, holding her mesmerized stare the entire time.

She couldn't hold a solid thought. Couldn't even work up a good, solid panic, she was so aroused and excited and — and maybe just that little bit afraid.

Or was worried a better word?

Her hands pulled instinctively at the ties binding her wrists, even though she didn't really want to get away. Her breathing became hard and heavy, sounding loudly in the quiet room, and then the warm tip of the Pyrex cock was pressed against her hole and, God help her, he was pushing it up into her, one hand holding her lips spread wide, the other working the thick glass into her, fucking her with it as if it were an extension of himself.

Ohmygod. Her pussy clenched around the warm glass, clamping down hard, and it was unbearably erotic the way Jake watched the entire thing, his eyes glued to her, his expression transfixed with lust as the thick glass moved in and out of her tight little opening.

"Oh hell," he growled into the breath filled silence. "You are so fucking sexy. Even when I used to jerk off thinking about doing this to you, I never imagined it'd be like this. Never knew it'd make me so fucking hot."

And it was obvious that it did. His massive cock was rising hard and high, infinitely more beautiful than the blue work of erotic art lodged in her core and a thousand times more dangerous to her senses. This was so much—too much—and she couldn't find herself in the rush of sensations pounding through her while Jake fucked her with this pretty blue cock. Then he was pulling it out of her, setting the wet, cream and oil covered glass on the bed beside his knee while he grasped her hips, flipping her to her stomach. Her cunt clenched in need, hating to be empty, and she looked back at him over her shoulder, her eyes widening to see him pouring the oil over his own cock this time, working it into his skin from root to tip.

Oh, shit, she thought, wondering if now would be a good time to start to worry. "Jake, um, what are you doing?"

He set the oil aside again, positioning himself between her spread thighs. "On your knees, baby."

She was moving without even thinking about it, obeying the command in his voice, while her mind still churned with breathless anticipation. "Jake—what are you going to do to me?"

His hands grasped the rosy cheeks of her ass, spreading them, fingertips rubbing oil into the tight little bud hidden between. Down lower her pussy was flooding, quivering, dripping down her thighs—betraying the fact that she was more than enjoying their little walk on the wild side here. Telling him he could do anything he wanted to her and she'd love it.

"I won't ever do anything to hurt you," he whispered roughly, suddenly pressing the huge tip of his cock against that tiny entrance, pushing until he somehow—somehow slipped inside with a strange popping sensation, feeling a thousand times bigger than his thumb had.

"Oh, fuck, fuck, fuck," he growled again and again, fingers digging into her waist, his hips working back and forth, nudging him into the tight channel one thick increment at a time.

Sharp, shocked, hoarse cries spilled from her throat, her entire body going tense and tight, fighting the strange sensation—the searing penetration of his cock into a place she'd just never thought of as sexual. But as in everything else, Jake was teaching her—showing her that there was a hell of a lot more to her than she'd ever allowed set free. Or…maybe she'd just been waiting for the right man to release this sensual, erotic, wild woman living inside of her.

Jake curved himself over her, placing his head beside her ear, whispering darkly. "Relax, Taylor. Just breathe and let me in. You feel so good, so fucking incredible."

She whimpered as he pushed deeper, unable to deny that the strange penetration did feel wonderfully good in a dark, forbidden kind of way. Then he had one hand in front of her, the huge glass dildo in its grasp, and he was pressing it into the empty, dripping mouth of her pussy again. "Jake!" she cried, sobbing into the pillow. "Oh, Jesus— Jake!"

He pushed, working it into her tight channel, and then it was there, buried deep inside of her pussy while Jake filled her ass. They could both feel it, the full press of the blue glass inside of her, and he shuddered behind her, his cock leaping higher into her, pulling a strangled sound from her throat.

"Taylor," he groaned, the novel sensations surrounding his cock, beating against him with her pulse. "That feels so fucking amazing."

And it did. She felt so full, so penetrated, so taken. She tried to find herself in it, but he began moving, taking her with the glass, cramming it into her pussy with hard, slow thrusts mimicked by his beautiful cock—and the pleasure began to pump through her body strong and sweet and violent in its intensity.

She almost had the rhythm when she felt him change his grip on the end so that he could twist the blue cock inside of her—a new shock of sensation spearing right through her sex-ravaged core.

Oh, God, she thought, it's going to kill me. It's so good it's going to kill me!

And then suddenly she couldn't think of anything at all because he was driving every rational thought from her mind with the pull and press of his cock and hands. They were shaking and shouting, grinding together in an orgy of flesh and need and ecstasy, sweat flying from their burning bodies as they came together in a way that was almost vicious in its intensity.

Somehow she braced her weight on her elbows—her hands still tied—and lifted her head till she could look at him over her shoulder. Almost in an instant, his mouth was there, capturing her own, and his wicked tongue was eating at her mouth, claiming this sweet orifice as thoroughly as he claimed the other two.

She was full of him—full of Jake.

Her body clenched so hard he shouted into her mouth, forcing the sound down her throat, and then she was coming all over him, hard and wet and tight, while her cunt drenched his fingers and the glass, and her tongue tangled with his own. It pulled his own orgasm right out of him, ripped it from his very soul, and he pumped his hips in an aggressive rhythm while filling that tight little hole with pulsing jets of cum, saturating them with it.

They collapsed with a hard thud against the sweat and oil soaked sheets, breathing hard and fast and feeling as if they'd experienced death in a wildly chaotic storm of pleasure. As carefully as he could, Jake pulled his cock and their drenched blue toy out of her still pulsing body, then clumsily reached up to untie her wrists.

When she was free, she rolled to her side, groaning from the shuddering sensations still pumping through her system, and he pulled her into his strong arms, holding her so tightly she could barely breathe.

Taylor lost the concept of time, unsure how long they lay there, hearts pounding and lungs working, before a wicked, delight-filled giggle worked its way up out of her throat. "Jake," she groaned, laughing and crying all at the same time, "I think you killed me."

He smiled against the top of her head, holding her tighter, amazed by the heights he could find with this woman. "I think I've killed us both," he moaned playfully, kissing her scalp. "But you loved it, sugar."

She snuggled into him, rubbing her nose against his silky chest hair. "Have you really never done that kind of thing before?"

"Never, sweetheart. I was as innocent as a virgin. Are you shocked?"

"I'm too dead to be shocked," she mumbled against his skin, but he could hear the teasing smile in her voice and knew that he'd pleased her with his admission.

"You've thoroughly corrupted me, honey. No more good little school boy, now that I've found my wild side, and you probably won't ever be able to walk straight again," he murmured, trailing his fingertips down the slender, sensual line of her back, "because I'll be fucking all your pretty little holes every chance I get. You're gonna be so tender, Taylor—and then I'll kiss you all better till you're ready to be thoroughly fucked all over again. And you'll have no one to blame but yourself."

"Hah!" she huffed dramatically, enchanted by this teasing side of him. "Don't blame me. I've never even read about anything like that, much less thought it up on my own. That was all your own sordid, diabolical fantasy, Mr. Farrell."

He laughed in her ear, a dark, sexy sound that said he knew she was full of shit. "Don't try to act like you didn't like it. I've got teeth marks in my lip to prove how much you loved it."

"I didn't say I didn't like it, but—" She rolled to her back, staring up into his rugged, outrageously sexy face as he propped himself up on an elbow beside her, his hair falling over his brow and his jaw dark with stubble again. "I think you owe me."

His brow arched, one fingertip teasing a line back and forth from the hollow of her throat to the shadowy indentation of her navel. "Have at me, sweetheart. I'm yours to do with as you please; whatever you have in mind."

She stretched luxuriously, feeling wonderfully alive. "Well, since I've done a first for you, now it's your turn."

He laughed darkly. "And that wasn't a first for you too?" he asked with another arched brow, the corner of his mouth lifting.

She batted her lashes. "Done it thousands of times, with thousands of men, if you must know the truth."

"I sure as hell hope not," he growled, leaning back on the pillows, watching her with new fire in his eyes. New? Hell, it never went away.

"Why?" she asked curiously, threading her fingers through her hair as she sat up, trying to restore it to some semblance of order but knowing it was hopeless.

His smile was wicked and mean, looking dark and piratical. "Because then I'd have to track them all down and kill their sorry asses."

"Hmm." She raised her own brow in imitation of his. "Sounds messy. I guess you're lucky I haven't left a string of lovers all over the country, then, aren't you?"

"I'm lucky to have you, Taylor," he replied in a low voice. It was gruff with feelings that he couldn't hide. Feelings he wasn't even trying to disguise. "And don't ever think for a second that I don't know it."

Chapter 15

His last comment was too much for her shattered emotions to take right now, and Taylor moved fast before she did something outrageously stupid, like throw her arms around the gorgeous man and tell him she'd loved him since the moment she'd set eyes on him at sixteen.

Yeah, that would be bad. But when she tried to scramble to her feet too quickly, intent on fleeing temptation, the look that fell over her face was almost comical—a mixture of surprise and embarrassment and stunned discovery. Her limbs were like Jell-O, a dull ache pounding between her legs, and she stumbled awkwardly with the first step she tried to take.

Jake was on his feet in an instant, his strong arms wrapping around her, lifting her easily, as if she weighed no more than a handful of feathers. "Oh hell," he drawled. "I broke you, didn't I?"

Taylor laughed softly against his chest as he carried her to the bathroom. "Not broken exactly, but I think I could definitely use some downtime."

He set her on her feet as he reached into the stall and started the water running hot, the small white room quickly filling with steam. "This'll help," he explained with his sexy smile, pulling her beneath the heavy spray of hot water. "Just close your eyes and relax, I'll take care of you."

She smiled, her eyes drifting closed, finding it easier to give over to him each time he demanded it. Between her self-absorbed mother and Mitch, she'd never had anyone who wanted to care for her before. She'd always been the one doing for others, but Jake lavished attention on her as if he not only wanted to do it, but needed to do it. It was as if he enjoyed caring for her, giving her the love and attention she'd never had but had always craved.

And yet, he didn't treat her like a china doll, something fragile and easily breakable, and she loved that most of all. Jake treated her like a woman. A very sexy, desirable woman that he couldn't keep his hands off of, that he couldn't get enough of, who made him continually loose control. What could be better than that?

Well, having him for a lifetime, of course, but she'd already made her decision on that point and she knew it was for the best. It may not be the one she wanted, or even the right one for that matter, but it was the only one she could live with. She couldn't risk becoming a bitter old hag full of jealousy and mistrust and hate, and she very much feared that was what she'd become if she tried to make a life with the gorgeous man slowly running his big, soap covered hands over her quivering pink body.

That was one lesson Mitch had taught her well, and she wasn't about to forget it. That did not, however, mean she couldn't wring as much pleasure as possible from the short time she still had with Jake, and there were only a handful of hours left. Her heart twisted with savage despair, and she threw her arms around him, holding tight, as if she could keep him forever by clinging to him now. A strangled sob worked its way up through her tight throat as his own strong arms wrapped around her, engulfing her in his warm embrace, holding her tightly like he never meant to let her go. His lips pressed against the sensitive part in her hair, brushing her scalp, and they held tighter, rocking slowly on their feet, lost in the moment.

Taylor lost all concept of how long they clung to one another beneath the hot spray of water, but when it began to run cold, Jake turned it off and quickly had her wrapped up tight in a large fluffy towel, carrying her back to the tumbled wreck of the bed. She luxuriated in the feeling of being held in his arms as he lay down beside her, feeling somehow cherished. Feeling—feeling loved, and her heart clenched harder from the ache of loss and insecurity.

She thought of his wonderful, heartbreaking words earlier in his truck, the amazing depth of emotion he'd claimed to have held for her when a young man, and the need to believe became a nearly unbearable pain. Then she hardened her jaw, swallowed down the ridiculous self-pity, and resolved to get her ass up and take advantage of the magnificent subject laid out beside her while she still had the chance.

"Enough stalling," she said sleepily, pulling out of the strong arms that were obviously reluctant to let her go. She stood beside the bed, staring down into his dark, questioning green eyes, for the first time in her life unashamed of her body. Though she still had plenty of doubts and insecurities, her desirability as a woman was no longer one of them. Not with the constant heat in those sexy green eyes as they watched her, the fire of lust always burning brightly for her to see. She smiled a sultry, siren smile as his eyes went darker, all green flaming light, fired with need. "Now it's my turn. No, don't move. Well, just shift to your side a bit. There—like that," she instructed while he positioned his big, beautiful body atop the sheets, clearly intrigued by what she had planned.

His eyes narrowed as she began digging through her art satchel, pulling out a thick tablet of expensive drawing paper and a stubby stick of dark gray charcoal. "What in the hell are you doing?" he grunted.

She smiled over her shoulder at him as she put her bag away. "I'm going to sketch you."

The brow went up again, not to mention more prominent parts. His gaze swept over his sprawled, thoroughly naked body. "Like this?"

"Yeah. I figure I ought to get it on paper, seeing as how I've got you all laid out and sexy and to myself. I need to preserve the memory for posterity." She flashed him a teasing smile. "My duty as an artist to womankind and all that."

The sudden look of panic on his face was almost comical. "No way in hell are you drawing pictures of my naked ass and then—" he ground his jaw, knowing he had to be careful about what he said here, "and then showing them to anyone, Taylor."

"Of course not," she laughed softly, positioning herself on the end of the bed near his feet, her eyes turning serious as they studied his mouthwatering form. "They're just for me."

He leaned back, slightly mollified. "You know, you don't need drawings of me for posterity, sweetheart, because I'm going to be glued to your side for the rest of your life." He hadn't used the "L" word again, so he wasn't really breaking her fucked up little condition on that score, but her answering smile was still brittle, and he could see the obstinate unwillingness to discuss their future in her eyes.

He wanted to yell and rage and shout at her until she got it through that thick little skull of hers that this was about forever, but maybe it still wasn't the right time. Or maybe he was just too chicken shit, afraid of what the outcome was going to be.

He tried to relax as he watched her work, wondering how she saw him, what she saw beyond the surface of his skin. That was the thing about Taylor's talent as an artist. She not only created works of beauty, but she captured a subject's soul, transferring life into a two dimensional medium. When you studied her art, even those drawings she'd done as a girl, you saw emotions, raging and passionate, and he'd often thought about them. Wondered if that was how she expressed her hidden feelings, how she gave them release.

Was her art her outlet for love? For pain? Regret?

And she was beautiful to watch as she worked. He loved her delicate breasts, the way they gently swayed as she began sketching, finding this whole setup more erotic than he could've ever imagined. It was a heady feeling, watching her watch him, the absorbed look in her big brown eyes, knowing she was studying every intimate detail of his body, transferring it into art with her awesome talent. His skin was burning, itching, aching to feel her against him again, as if only her touch could soothe the need burning beneath the surface. Though he really didn't mean to distract her, his eyes became glued to her puffy pink nipples, his tongue stroking the roof of his mouth, desperate for their taste and silky soft texture.

Taylor saw where he was looking and felt the traitorous buds go rock hard, spiking into the air, hungry for his touch.

Jake gave an answering smile that was soft and lazy, the knowing look in his hot, heavy-lidded eyes telling her without words he knew exactly how he affected her. Trying not to squirm, she picked up his blue twill shirt from where he'd thrown it on the floor earlier and slipped her arms into the soft fabric, its huge size engulfing her so that she didn't even need to button the front to be modestly covered. "Maybe you should, um, just close your eyes and try to relax for me."

He snuggled deeper into the pillows, lounging like a decadent pasha, obviously confident in his power and the irresistible appeal he held for her. Damn, Taylor figured she was lucky her tongue wasn't hanging out of her mouth. There was a sweet, tender ache between her legs, and she knew Jake felt it too because his cock was once again hard and throbbing, more than ready to fuck, as if they hadn't spent the day in a sexual orgy, feasting off one another, gorging on orgasms.

He eyed her now shirt-covered form as she picked up her pad and charcoal stick to begin sketching again, and drawled, "Spoilsport."

He knew she was trying to hide from him, but he didn't need to see her tender, naked body to hunger for it. Of course, if he had the option, he'd keep her bare-assed naked and ready to fuck twenty-four hours a day, but hey, he could be realistic. There were times when clothes would be necessary, but that didn't mean he couldn't tell her with his eyes how much he wanted what was underneath them. Taylor was too perfect to be so shy and uncomfortable in her own, beautiful skin, and he looked forward with hungry greed to a lifetime spent ridding her of those ridiculous insecurities.

He lay there on the sticky sheets that smelled sweetly of oil and sweat and cum, and let the love that he felt for this woman flow through him, filling his skin, pounding through his blood. His heart swelled with it as the volatile emotion washed through him. He felt his cock grow harder, his eyes burning, the surfeit of emotion all but glowing from his skin. And she watched him from beneath her lashes, head lowered in concentration while her small hand flew over the paper with awe-inspiring ease and speed.

Jake thought of all the times over the years when she'd stood before her easel and pictured him in her mind, creating him from oils and imagination, and his heart twisted for all the years they'd lost, aching for the need to fill her future with himself. He'd be happy to let her draw him or paint him or do whatever the hell she wanted to do to his sorry ass for the rest of his life, so long as she would promise to stay with him forever. Hell, he'd stand on his fucking head and bark like a dog if that's what it took to make her happy.

All she had to do was name it and it was hers—his body, his heart, his soul. They already belonged to her; he just had to find the way to convince her to claim them.

He pulled one arm behind his head, muscles bulging, arm pit dark and wonderfully decorated with hair as black as that on his head, the other stroking his hard stomach while he mulled it over, thinking it through.

She watched as his big hand moved over his bare skin in a hypnotic rhythm that made her want to drool.

Bad sign, Taylor. A woman getting ready to drool is not a woman with the willpower to say no.

"Do you know how many times I've woken in the middle of a wet dream — dreaming about fucking you?" he asked into the silence of their breathing and charcoal moving over paper.

Taylor looked up at him over the edge of the tablet, and her eyes went smoky at the sight of his large hand wrapping around his even larger cock, moving slowly from the wide base up over the thick, glistening tip. Up and down his hand went, her eyes greedily following its every movement, and she nearly swallowed her tongue.

He pulled his other hand out from behind his head and reached over for the oil, bringing it to the tip of his cock, spilling the gleaming liquid over the head until it dribbled down the sides of his shaft, syrupy and golden in the soft lamplight.

"N-n-no," she stammered breathlessly, watching his hand working up and down, spreading the oil, pumping him bigger, fuller, until it looked like he'd burst at any moment. But his other hand gripped the base of his cock again, holding back the cum, and she just kept staring, finding the sinful sight too sexy to resist.

"Come here," he growled, his deep voice biting with demand.

His hand pumped harder, his cock engorged on blood and lust, and she marveled at how that magnificent thing ever fit inside of her. Her pussy, already swollen and wet, began creaming between her thighs, demanding to be filled. And she knew exactly what she wanted to fill it with. Tossing pad and charcoal to the floor, she shrugged out of his shirt and went to all fours between his feet, perched and ready to pounce. "You must be feeling pretty lucky, Mr. Farrell. I don't usually do this sort of thing with my models."

"Come up here," he grunted, "and I'll show you just how lucky I feel."

She went willingly into his arms, their bodies coming together with a keen anticipation for the joining of their flesh. It was a craving that grew each time, a hunger that demanded more each time it fed.

His mouth found hers, eating with a desperate, yet gentle avidity as he guided her charcoal-covered hands over his body, needing to feel her touch as strongly as he needed to touch her own naked flesh.

Her thighs parted for him eagerly as he moved her onto her back, and he slid between them, his cock probing then seeking entrance, working itself back into her with a ruthless possession, while his mouth never left hers. Long, slow drugging kisses that devastated her senses as thoroughly as the feel of his cock within her pulsing, liquid pussy — two unhurried and deep and deliberate penetrations. One hand curved around her hip, holding her to him, while the other stroked down her side, savoring the feel of her skin, the lean lines of her delicate body.

Jake wasn't fucking her this time; he was making love to her. His body was a knowing instrument of torture, driving his point home with each grinding stroke of his hips against her own, with each exquisite thrust of his cock within her juice-soaked cunt. The bite of his fingers into her delicate skin told her of his need for her, the passion that raged in his blood for no other woman but her.

And all the while he held her eyes, the smoldering look burning there telling her everything she refused to hear. It was all there, staring her right in the face, demanding she acknowledge its existence until it became too much for them and they tumbled helplessly over the edge, grinding together in a release that was softer than those that had come before, but in no way less fantastic. It was a slow, burning, throbbing pulse of pleasure, and they drank down the other's cries of ecstasy like fine wine, heady with sensation.

Somehow Jake managed to roll to his side, keeping her pinned to him, his cock still clasped in her slow pulsing sex, and they drifted into sleep sealed together. He awoke sometime later in the night, miraculously hard again, still inside of her, and took them both to the edge with a slow, gentle fuck that felt like hot, dripping honey.

Holding her hip, he moved her to her back without breaking contact, his ruthless cock digging inside of her, tearing low groans out of them both. Gathering her small body beneath him, they melted together, their mouths fused as intimately as their sexes. Her breasts crushed achingly against his chest, their hearts pounding one with the other.

Jake could just make out her delicate features in the soft glow of the moon. She looked beautiful and thoroughly ravished. "Hell, this has been a crazy time for you, hasn't it?"

She loved him all the more for the worry and regret she could hear in his voice. Stupid man. Like he didn't know he'd given her everything she'd ever dreamed of. Well, almost everything. He'd tried to offer more, but it just wasn't in her to be able to believe. And as much as she wished it were otherwise, she knew Jake Farrell wasn't a forever kind of guy.

Fighting back those dreadful tears, she smiled and said, "It's been wonderful and you know it."

Their eyes met. Held. His mouth twisted with a wry smile, and he murmured, "Did you ever feel this with Mitch?"

She stared up at him in the watery darkness, wondering why he wanted to know. For all the wonderfully possessive remarks he'd made during the long hours they'd spent together, she still couldn't bring herself to accept that he actually meant any of it. So then why was he still so curious about her marriage?

Trying to make light of the question, she forced a small laugh. "If he'd ever made me feel even a fraction of the way you do, Jake, I probably wouldn't have had the willpower to leave him."

She felt the slight tightening of muscle along his body, her breath catching as the next of his now grinding thrusts forced him impossibly deep, as if reminding her that he was the one buried deep inside of her now. Then he lowered his head and kissed her parted lips. "I hate the thought that he was your first. That he ever had you, because he never deserved you, Taylor. Never."

She took a deep breath and did the unthinkable, unable to stop herself. "What was it like? The first time you made love to a woman?"

Color burned hot beneath his sun-bronzed flesh, the silky skin stretched taut over high cheekbones. His eyes glittered, as dark as infinite space in the moonlight. Green ice. She loved the crinkles at their corners. The grooves that bracketed his sinful mouth. All the delicious details that made him the man he was.

"This is it, Taylor." His mouth pressed against her own again, then trailed kisses down her throat to rest against the hollow at its base. "This is the first time I've ever made love to a woman."

He pushed even deeper then, and she felt the passion, the need, rolling through him like a cresting wave; a ripple and flex of muscle and bone that could have terrified her if she didn't trust him to keep her safe. Jake felt it surge through him and gave himself over to it for another first. They rode it together, letting it carry them through to its devastating rush of ecstasy and pulsating crescendo.

When they came, he felt tears fall hotly from her eyes, streaming down her cheeks. He licked them dry with the velvet rasp of his tongue, understanding their source because the same shattering emotions rocked through him as well. Sleep eventually claimed them again, in the quiet moonlight of the night—and in the morning, she was gone.

Chapter 16

The scraping wail of a siren was the last thing Jake wanted to hear. He was so fucking furious, he didn't trust himself not to take it out on good ol' Sheriff Mitch McCarter and beat the ever-loving hell outta him.

Taylor had run out on him.

He couldn't believe it—couldn't get his head around it. Fifteen minutes ago, he'd awakened to an empty hotel room smelling of sex and Taylor and cum. He didn't know what the stubborn-ass woman was thinking, but she was out of her ever-loving mind if she thought they were finished. Hah! He was going to spend the rest of his life loving her silly and still not be finished with her sweet little ass.

He was so panicked he could barely breathe, wondering what hare-brained reason she had for ditching him. Surely she didn't think he'd gotten his fill of her. He'd told her he loved her—and he sure as hell knew she loved him.

She always had.

The painful blare of the siren snapped his attention back to the moment. Jake flashed his eyes to the rearview mirror and smashed his hand on the steering wheel. Fuck, this was all he needed. He pulled to the side of the road and climbed out of his truck so they could get this over and done with and he could be on his way. As he watched

Mitch climb out of the Bronco, he flexed his fingers, fighting the urge to give into his anger.

Mitch took off his mirrored sunglasses as he leaned back against the hood of the Bronco, staring out of lifeless, bloodshot eyes. Jake barely recognized him. His once golden head of hair was now streaked with gray, the rough features of his once handsome face now etched with tired resignation. Whatever spirit his childhood friend had possessed, Jake could see it had long ago shriveled up and died. Mitch looked far older than his years, as if he'd lived too fast in the beginning and was now buried beneath the backlash of time. Then again, he'd probably just gone sour on hate and bitterness.

After several tension filled moments, Mitch's mouth curled with a sneer. "You fucked her, didn't you?"

Jake had no intention of relaying any of the details of his and Taylor's relationship to anyone. And it was definitely a relationship, whether the idiot woman realized it or not. She'd given herself to him and he was keeping her, end of story. To Mitch, he simply flashed a cocky smile and drawled, "Nice to see you too, Sheriff McCarter."

Mitch's long, lanky body vibrated with rage. His hands fisted at his sides, his shoulders bunched. "Cut the crap, Farrell. Wanda told me all about your little show the other day. You came back just to screw around with Taylor, didn't you? Couldn't wait to show up and fuck her the way you always wanted to."

Jake took an aggressive step forward, pointing a finger in Mitch's angry face. "I'll take a lot of shit from you Mitch because you were my friend once and because you've become such a pathetic bastard now, but I'll pound the shit out of you if you so much as mention Taylor's name again. You got that?"

Mitch jerked straight, mottled with fury. "Who in the hell do you think you are?" he exploded, thumping his chest with his fist. "She's my wife!"

"No. She's not. You blew your shot, Mitch. You know it as well as I do. That's why you're so pissed. You had the best woman in the world and you threw her away. Tough shit for you, pal, because now you're just going to have to live with it."

Mitch snorted. "Hell," he muttered, his voice thick with disgust. "I never had her to begin with. She was always so strung up on you. It made me sick, all those friggin' paintings and crap." He turned around, smashing his fist down on the Bronco's battered hood. "Hell, she used to moan your name in her sleep at night. Drove me outta my fuckin' mind."

If Mitch thought Jake was capable of feeling any pity for him, he was sadly mistaken. Whatever hell Mitch lived in had been of his own choosing. If he hadn't meddled in their lives ten years ago, spreading his vicious lies and trying to turn Taylor against him, they'd have been married for years now and Mitch might've had the chance to find someone who really loved him. But he'd tried to trap Taylor for his own, and caused the three of them years of misery in the process.

"I'm not gonna feel bad about that, Mitch, because you never deserved her. Even while you had her, you treated her like shit, when you knew she was the best thing to ever happen to you."

Mitch hung his head forward between his shoulders, his fists still clenched on the hood of the truck. Jake didn't know if he was going to take a swing at him or not, and he really didn't care. Yeah, it'd feel good to knock his teeth down his throat, but it wasn't going to change things. And being stuck with the likes of Wanda Merton almost seemed like punishment enough.

Almost—but it'd still feel good to pound the crap outta him.

"So now what? You just gonna screw her till you're through with her? Shove my face in it, is that it?"

"No. I'm going to marry her."

Mitch took a deep, trembling breath, and then another. Finally he just stood up and walked to his door, pulling it open. With his sunglasses back in place, he turned to face the man who'd once been like a brother to him. "I always knew this shit was gonna happen someday," he laughed, but the hoarse sound held more miserable regret than humor. "You always did get every damn thing you wanted. Wasn't a girl in Westin who'd tell you no."

"Yeah, but I would've traded every one of them for just one minute with Taylor. I love her, Mitch. You know I always have."

Mitch snorted again, then just shook his blonde head as he climbed up into his seat. Suddenly, he couldn't understand how he'd ever gotten to this point in life. "You're still an arrogant fuck, you know that?"

Jake flashed a cocky smile. "Yeah? Why else would we ever have been friends?"

The Bronco's engine cranked to life. For a brief moment, the thought flashed through Jake's mind that Mitch might be crazy enough to run him over. He laughed at himself as his muscles tensed, like he was going to have a chance in hell if Mitch went fucking nuts on him, but the Bronco pulled into the road and stopped. Through the open passenger's side window, Mitch said, "I don't suppose I have to tell you to get the hell outta town?"

"Shit," Jake drawled, knowing this was Mitch's strange ass way of saying goodbye. "Like you could pay us to stay."

He watched the Bronco pull away, feeling like he'd just closed that last remaining door to his past. For the first time in his entire adult life, he was looking forward to his future, instead of behind him.

There was just one remaining detail.

He needed to go and grab hold of the woman who made him whole.

And this time, he wasn't letting her out of his sight.

Chapter 17

Because of his run in with Mitch, Taylor had already showered by the time Jake was pounding his fist on her front door, all but shaking the frame of the house. When she opened it, she was fresh and sweet smelling, with her long hair damp around her flushed face.

His chest clenched tight. It was nuts, the things this woman did to him. He wanted to roll himself all over her until he'd marked her with his scent again, wanted her claimed as his in the most basic, elemental way two animals could connect. He wanted her to smell like him, coated in his cum, with her own juices smeared all over his body.

He'd never felt so savagely primitive before, like a red raging beast of possessiveness. And what made it human was the heart buried beneath the lust. The heart that wanted to be claimed just as strongly as it wanted to conquer. The human heart married with the needs of the flesh, secured by love and trust and commitment. Shit, he was waxing poetic here, but there was no help for it. Any moment now he was going to be on his knees begging, and he figured he might as well get it said right the first time.

Then the crazy woman had the nerve to say, "Jake, what are you doing here?" His noble intentions flew right out the window. Wild man surged forward in all his ruthless glory, and he knew she could see it in his eyes, the set of his mouth. She stepped back, moved away from him, but at least she didn't slam the door in his face. Jake stalked into the house before she changed her mind.

She kept backing up, but he just kept moving in on her. He took a step toward her, then another, advancing with the predatory skill of a dark, dangerous animal preparing to strike. Her eyes were swollen and red, as if she'd been crying, and the sight ripped a tear of pain right through him. He reached her in three long strides, backing her against the wall, pinning her there with the delicious strength of his long, muscle-hard body. She trembled as he cupped her cheek, holding her in place with his legs braced on either side of her own.

His eyes searched hers, desperate for answers. "Why'd you run out on me, Taylor?"

She bit her lip, trying to stop its ridiculous trembling. She wasn't afraid of Jake. She was afraid of herself—afraid of making an absolute fool of herself over him. Each time he'd come into her, he'd taken a little more away when he withdrew. He'd possessed her, staked a claim, and her mind had recognized the fact as clearly as her body. If she'd stayed another day, there wouldn't have been any fight left in her and she would have given in. She'd have given him anything he wanted, including her heart, and even though it'd always belonged to him, she still couldn't find the strength to acknowledge his claim.

That was why she'd run, fleeing like a coward. One short taxi ride home, and she'd thought she'd cut her ties to him forever.

She was holding the pain tight to her chest like a bitter old woman living off of fear and worry and regret. She was too young to have even lived her life yet and here she was, already throwing it away because she was too terrified to take a chance on love. It was pathetic, and she hated herself for this inherent weakness and insecurity.

She tried for a smile, but knew she failed big time. "Come on, Jake. Did you really want me there this morning? You got—what you wanted." She shrugged, swallowing down the uneasy pain. "I didn't see the point in going through an awkward goodbye."

His hand moved from her cheek, back into her hair, fingers spearing through the silken mass to hold her in place. "Jesus, you just don't get it, do you, woman? I didn't come back to settle some old score with Mitch, you little idiot. And I didn't come back just to get your sweet ass in the sack, though God knows that's exactly where I want it, every single day and night. I came back for a hell of a lot more than that, Taylor."

Her lips thinned, eyes suddenly flaring with fury. "And you thought what, Jake? That I was just going to run from one womanizing bastard to another?" She crossed her arms, hugging them against her body in a desperate attempt to hold herself together. "Give me a little more credit than that. I know what men like you want. Variety, Jake. Lots and lots of variety."

The sound that burst from his throat was part outrage, part laughter. "Hell, he really did a number on you, didn't he, babe? You don't have a fuckin' clue what kind of man I am. Not if you can compare me to Mitch. Mitch is a spineless, sniveling coward. That's why he ran around screwing any and every damn thing that moved. He knew he wasn't man enough for you, Taylor, and he blew the best thing in his life because he was so afraid of losing it."

"To who, Jake? You expect me to believe Mitch has been worrying about the day you'd come back to town?" she scoffed, finding the idea too ridiculous to even credit.

"That's why he threw our marriage away? Because he knew you were going to come back for me? He was just waiting to get screwed over, so he screwed me over instead?"

"Damn straight. And he was right. Not that your marriage had a chance in hell of lasting anyway, because you married the wrong guy, sweetheart. I already knew I'd wasted enough time waiting for you to come to your senses. When my uncle called, I was already on my way here. I already had my bags packed, Taylor."

"And you knew I'd just be waiting here with open arms? How, Jake? What'd you do, read my mind from thousands of miles away?"

Green sparks of passion lit his eyes, his mouth going grim with determination. "No, I read your book. All of them, actually."

Taylor groaned, mortified all the way down to her toes. Oh, God. It was like a great gaping hole opening at her feet. He'd looked and seen just how obsessed with him she'd always been. Rainier, her King of the Faeries, was the spitting image of Jake, as were Nashtash the Warlock and Ivanor the Gaul. God, she wanted to crawl into a little ball on the floor and die right then and there.

How was she going to explain this one without coming right out and admitting that she'd been more than just attracted to him all this time? It was too much, after everything else she'd so stupidly 'fessed up to. She couldn't take it. This was supposed to have been all about sex for him, wasn't it? Scratching an old itch and all that. Why was he trying to turn it into more?

His body pressed closer, cutting off any chance of escape. "I've seen them all, sweetheart. One day I was cruising through this Barnes and Noble and there you were. A picture of you and your pretty little books spread out all around it. I bought every single one of them. That was six months ago, and I've pored over them every day since then trying to figure out what they meant. When I finally thought I'd got it, I came back. And one look at you told me I'd been right."

"Well hooray for you, Jake. I'm sure that's just what your enormous ego needed, more fuel for the fire." She squeezed her eyes shut and let her head bang back against the wall, thankful for the distracting pain. God, she couldn't look at him. She must seem so pathetic to someone as strong as Jake—like a broken little waif too homely for anyone to want, aching for love from someone as gorgeous and sexy and vibrant as him. He was all the bold colors she'd ever painted him with, while she was small and washed out.

Invisible.

Transparent.

She could feel his stare like a lick of fire across her skin. She was shivering, but she wasn't cold. Maybe it was that strange tremble that came before shock. Any second now and her world would go mercifully black. It was so odd, like floating, if only Jake would stop shaking her shoulders, demanding her attention.

"Taylor, don't you dare pass out on me. Take a deep breath and open your damn eyes, woman."

Tiny pinpricks of cold were dancing against the backs of her lids, across the tingling flesh of her lips. "I can't," she moaned. "This is so horrible. Please, Jake. Just leave me alone."

"Like hell I will," he growled. "What do you think I'm going to do, Taylor? Laugh at you? Make fun of you? Don't you know what I saw when I opened those books and found my own fucking face staring back at me from every single page, over and over again? Don't you?"

He didn't wait for her to answer, just pressed his mouth against her own and ate his way inside. His head moved from one angle to another, its only intention to get deeper inside that sweet, moist recess till he'd touched and tasted every part of it. It was a consuming kiss. Hungry and demanding, worshipping her mouth with pleasure. And she was right there with him, pulling him in, stroking his tongue with the hungry need of her own.

No one, she thought. There couldn't be anyone else in the entire world that kissed the way Jake Farrell did. It was as if he were making love to her mouth, the same way she'd felt when he'd spent all those long, drugging moments with his head pressed between her legs—with his cock claiming possession of her pussy.

When he had to come up for air, he kept his lips against hers, unwilling to break the physical contact. "It made me crazy," he growled against them. "Drove me out of my mind to see those books because I knew you'd been just as crazy for me all these miserable fucking years. I knew it, Taylor. It was painted right there on every single friggin' page, screaming that you loved me. That you loved me, damn it, and I'd left you here! I'd left you with that lying bastard when you belonged with me!"

"I didn't need you to come back home and rescue me, Jake. I was doing just fine without you."

His hand bracketed her jaw, forcing her to hold his heated stare. "Is that right?"

She gave a jerky nod, and his grip tightened. "Well, I'm not buying it, sugar. I think you've been dying for the day I'd come back—because I know I sure as hell have been. You may not need me for anything, Taylor, but I need you for everything. I need you to make me complete, to make me whole—to make me stop feeling like half of a man! You're gonna have to let the baggage go, Taylor. I came back for you, and I'm not fucking leaving without you!"

Oh God. Something beautiful clicked free inside of her—the lock around her heart forced open—and she gasped or cried out, too overcome to recognize the noises tearing from her soul, pouring into his. Suddenly it seemed as if her life was about to find its defining moment in all its shining glory, right here in the arms of the only man she could ever love. "Jaaaake," she moaned, wrapping her arms around him, trying to crawl into his body, right through his skin. "Jake—"

His fingers twisted into her hair, tilting her face up to his. Their eyes met, both glassy with tears, stormy and violent and full of love. "I love you, Taylor. That's what I've been trying to show you. Trying to make you understand. I love you! Hell, I always have. I always will."

Jesus, he made her feel so strong. Jake wasn't bad for her. He believed in her, maybe enough for the both of them, and Taylor suddenly began to open her eyes to what was standing right in front of her.

She shuddered in his arms and tried to pull his mouth back against hers, but he wasn't finished. "Now tell me why you stayed. What were you waiting for? Tell me, Taylor. I need to hear it!"

"You!" she cried, holding him as tightly as he held her. "Oh, God, Jake, I was waiting for you! I always have been. I love you...I love you...I love you—"

That was the key he'd been waiting for to set the hunger free. It took only ten frenzied seconds of ripping at the buttons on his fly, dragging her skirt and panties out of the way, and then he was shoving her legs open with his own and knifing up into her, having to work against the swollen tissues of her sex-ravaged pussy until they finally relented and hugged him deep once more.

He plowed up into her, going straight and fast and thick.

She screamed as he pounded her into the wall, too caught up in everything to be gentle or seducing. Not that that was what she wanted. She wanted this—this wild, rough claiming that told her in no uncertain terms exactly who she belonged to.

And yet, it was as giving as it was taking. The long, thick thrusts of his body cramming itself into hers with such desperate need were proof of everything she needed to know. It was all there—hers for the taking, if she'd just reach out for it.

When he could finally find his voice, Jake grunted, "Then marry me, Taylor. Make me the happiest bastard alive and tell me you'll marry me."

"What?"

He ripped her shirt open, pulling her bra out of the way so he could lick her nipple, using all the weapons at his disposal, cheating like hell as he nibbled the pink tip with his teeth. He knew he should've waited to ask it, but he couldn't. He wanted it too badly.

"You heard me. Marry me," he demanded gruffly, his arms tightening in case she tried to pull away. Shit, he didn't want to scare her off by forcing his hand, but he'd been waiting a lifetime for this woman. What in the hell was the point in waiting any longer?

"You can't—you can't be serious."

Jake pulled back, looking down into her shocked face. Her eyes were huge, glistening with tears. He rubbed his thumb against her lower lip, marveling at the soft, silky texture, like the petal of a flower, only sweeter. "Don't give me that shit. You know I'm serious. I've never asked a woman to marry me before, and I sure as hell wouldn't do it as a joke."

She closed her eyes, wanting to be able to take this next leap with him, but cautious of it all the same. "I can't, Jake. I'd love to, but I just can't."

He went still inside of her. "Why the fuck not?"

"Because marriage is about love and commitment and trust, and we—we don't have those things. Not—not all of them."

He regarded her with serious eyes, his cock pressing deep, holding her there, impaling her. "You gonna fuck around on me? Let other guys shove their cocks up your pussy like this instead of me? Come down their throats? Suck 'em dry?"

The color drained from her face. "Of course not! How could you even think such a thing?"

One big hand bracketed her jaw again, demanding she hold his frustrated glare. "Yeah, well I think it sounds just as ridiculous. What in the hell would I go fucking around with some other woman for when I've got you? I'm not an idiot, Taylor. I'd rather cut my cock off than screw anyone but you ever again."

"God, now I know you can't be serious!"

He trapped her hands, raising them above her head, holding her captive against the wall. "Look at my face and see just how serious I am. I'll never fuck around on you, Taylor, and I mean that. More importantly, I'd never even want to. I'm not a man to make promises that I can't keep—that I don't want to keep. Do you understand that? The only woman I could ever make this promise to is you because you're the only one I want."

"But you don't want to marry me, Jake."

"Yeah?" he asked with his crooked smile, kissing her softly, rocking against her, confident in his victory. "Who says?"

"Well, you, that's who." The small crease between her arched brows was back in place, revealing her confusion. "Not once have you ever mentioned marriage before."

"Yeah? I thought I just did."

Her eyes narrowed. "I mean before now. Before today."

"Taylor, you little innocent," he laughed softly, "I never would've been able to fuck you nonstop for two days straight if I didn't love you, baby. I never would have asked you to marry me if I didn't love you. You understand that? Marriage is what I've wanted from you all along. It's what I came here for."

"But—"

"Taylor, of course I want to marry you. Hell, I thought you already understood that when I told you I love you. It's not some kind of puppy love, honey. I love you with everything I have, everything I am."

"Do you really, Jake?" Her voice was thick with wonder, eyes going glassy.

"Damn straight I do. I'm nothing without you, Taylor. I've just been a walking shell, waiting for our moment to come, and when I saw those books, I knew it was here and it was like my heart started beating for the first time. Fuck, it may sound corny as hell, but it's true."

"It's not corny," she hiccupped, smiling around her tears. "It's beautiful."

She looked up at the man before her — the man who'd always owned her heart — and suddenly understood it. Jake was hers and he always would be. The same violent passion and love that bound her to him, claimed him for her own. It worked both ways.

Jake would never betray her.

And he would never stop loving her.

She knew these things with her soul, but he gave her the words as well, even though she no longer needed them. As his body began to drive itself inside of hers, his talented cock forcing pleasure into the deepest recesses of her womb, he told her everything.

"I love you, Taylor. Always, baby. I love your mind and your spirit and this sweet little body that makes me hard just thinking about sinking into it. I love the way you taste. The way your warm, wet little cunt gushes for me, all sticky and sweet, begging to be fucked. I love the way it holds me tighter than anything I could've ever imagined. You were made for me, Taylor. Made for this. I'll never leave you or betray or hurt you, and I'm gonna spend the rest of my life trying to make you happy."

"You already do," she panted, feeling the tremors begin to tighten deep within, then ripple their way out until they were gripping his cock in a strong, delicious rhythm that nearly brought him to his knees. "God, just looking at you makes me happy. Just seeing your face. You're the most beautiful person I've ever known, Jake, inside and out."

"Yeah?" he whispered with a wealth of satisfaction, scraping his teeth across the silky mound of her breast. She squealed, wrapping her arms around his neck, nearly choking him. "You got something to say to me, woman?"

"I love you, Jake. I've always loved you. Always!" She smacked kisses all over his face, making him laugh and rub against her, their lovemaking turning playful one moment, incendiary the next.

"Taylor," he groaned, knowing there wasn't anything in the world as sweet as being buried up to your balls in the woman you loved with your very life. They wanted to savor the moment forever, but could no longer speak as the waves of pleasure crashed into them, throwing their bodies together with the raging force of the sea. She shouted with savage ecstasy, the erotic sound echoed by his own rough, animal-like growls, and they flooded into one another. He filled her up with a raging stream of cum, pouring in his love, while she bathed him in drenching wetness, coating him with it.

Sealed together, they floated slowly back to the moment, but reality was still rose-tinted and sweet. They saw through love-filled eyes, and the world would never look the same again.

"I love you, Taylor Nicole Moore. I always have." He wrapped himself around her, holding her so tight, with so much love. "God, I always will."

Their faces nuzzled like two kittens, their mouths curious, taking tiny licks and bites of the other's flesh. He nipped the delicate line of her jaw. She licked the salty skin beneath his ear, then tongued the sensitive shell. He shuddered, and neither were surprised that he remained full and firm inside of her. They had ten long, lonely years to make up for, and it was going to take the rest of their lives to do it right.

She was sore, but she didn't care. She loved the need she could feel in him. Loved the hunger she could feel in the way his cock buried itself so deep inside of her. He was too big to ever take comfortably, but she knew she'd always take him greedily. Jake was right. Her body had been made for this, made for him.

And the need was still riding her high, hungry for more, needing it now. "Jake, fuck me hard again. Please," she moaned. "I need to come again."

He smiled against her mouth. "You'll get your cock, beautiful. Every inch of it," he rasped in her ear, pressing deeper, reminding her just how much he had to give. "But I'm waiting for my answer. Stop being cruel."

She laughed, and it was a sound unlike any she'd ever made before. The laugh of a satisfied woman who knows she is loved and always will be. "I'm sorry," she teased against his throat, nipping at his warm, silky skin, loving his taste. "It's your fault, you know. You're distracting me."

His own laugh was dark and deep, causing his cock to surge further within, hitting that magic sweet spot that made her go all liquid and hot. Man oh man. "Get used to it, sweetheart. You're just going to have to learn to think with my cock buried deep, breaking open your sweet little pussy because that's where it plans on spending all its time."

"Hmm—and what about when I have to work?"

His hand delved between her legs, stroking the rim of her cock-full pussy, loving the way she stretched so tight around him. "I'll just bend you over your easel and fuck you from behind. You remember how that felt? How deep and full?" He licked her ear; bit the side of her neck. "I'm gonna fuck you like that all the time, Taylor. Just bend you over and fill you so full of cock you won't be able to see straight. It'll be so sweet, won't it, honey?"

"Mmmm—yes," she moaned, tightening her muscles until he gasped, a strong tremor moving through his tall, muscular body.

He growled. An actual growl. "An answer, Taylor. Give it to me now, before I lose my head and we go over all over again." He nudged deeper still, hitting that spot again, and she cried out sharp and raw. "I want to know you're going to be my wife before I fill you full of cum. I need to know it!"

"Oh, Jake," she giggled, looking up at him with an expression so soft and full of love he could only marvel at its beauty. "Of course I'll marry you. I love you, don't I?" She smoothed his eyebrows, sifted her fingers through the glossy strands of his dark hair. "Like you even had to ask."

He was smiling like an idiot as he kissed her, shaking with piercing relief, flooded with tenderness. "Of course I had to. I'm never taking you for granted, baby. Not a single moment I spend with you, and sure as hell not this. So get used to it, woman. From now on, you have a new pastime."

She gave an adorable snort that was somehow completely feminine. "You mean the one you told Wanda about?"

"Uh-huh. That's how it's gonna be. All the time. All you have to worry about is getting drenched so I can make you come, over and over and over. And I've got a whole lifetime of ideas, honey. Every way you can imagine, just waiting for you. I'm gonna spend the rest of my life making you so happy, you're going to walk around with a fuckin' glow."

"Oh yeah? And what about you?"

Jake licked at her lips, dipping inside to tease with his tongue. "Look at me, Taylor. Just seeing you makes me shine. You fucking set me on fire." His thumb brushed her clit, his fingers sliding down again to caress the rim of her overstretched opening as it swallowed him whole, loving the feel of his possession. "And no one'll own this sweet little cunt but me, right?"

"So long as that huge thing you call a cock belongs to me."

"It's yours," he grunted, pulling out, and shoving all those long, thick inches back into her cream soaked core. "I'm never gonna even look at another woman. I mean that, Taylor. Trust me."

"Good, 'cause you're mine now."

His thumb stroked her clit again, sending shivers all the way down to her toes, and his cock kept surging deeper, out and in, filling and stretching her with feelings too good to endure. She felt the contractions coming, the start of a roaring climax, and gripped his driving hips with her thighs, begging for more.

"Tell me how you want it, baby, and I'll make you come. Tell me to fuck your beautiful little cunt until you explode all over me."

She shut her eyes, head thrashing from side to side as she pleaded, "I can't, Jake. God, just make me—just make me—"

"Not good enough, Taylor. I wanna hear you say it."

Her face broke into a soft, sultry smile. "Hmm...I think I'm embarrassed again."

A growl rumbled in his throat. "You won't be for long."

She squeezed him to her, hiding her face in the hollow of his throat, surrounded by his rugged masculinity. "Not that a sensible woman could say no to such an offer, but do you think we could throw some babies in here somewhere? I do write children's books, you know. And I love kids."

"Aw, honey," he drawled, nudging her head up so he could look into her suddenly shy eyes, like she was actually worried about his answer. "A family's a given, Taylor. It always has been. I can't think of anything sexier than you all ripe and round with my baby. Shit, we'll probably have a dozen at least."

"A dozen!" she choked, sputtering, unsure if he was teasing or not.

"Yeah," he murmured, his eyes going dark with the thought. His cock flexed inside of her, clearly excited. "Let's start right now."

Taylor squirmed against him, sticky and wet. Her smile was pure seduction, wanton and teasing, making the knot in his dick triple with need. He went even thicker inside of her, impossibly harder at the thought of making her pregnant.

And she could feel it. The knowledge of her power glowed from within, illuminating her eyes and skin. She touched her tongue to the bow of her mouth, and Jake wanted to beg for mercy right then and there. "I take it this means I can trash my birth control pills?"

Jake groaned like a man in pain, or an agony of sensation. "Oh hell, I'm gonna kill myself loving you. You do know that, don't you?"

Taylor shifted her hips, taking him deeper, sucking him in, keeping him warm and safe and wet. "That's fine, Jake. Just take me with you." Her head fell back as she offered herself up with total abandon. "Just fuck me and take me with you. And you better make it good, big guy."

He groaned and laughed and shuddered as he pulled out and rammed back in, slamming her with his eager cock, the happiest man alive. "You got it, Taylor. We're on our way."

And they never looked back.

Epilogue

Today was his fiftieth birthday, and the house was full with family and friends. For the moment, Jake sat out in the back garden with his oldest son, Caleb, watching the waves ripple across the lake as Taylor put the final decorations on his birthday cake. He shifted and looked over his shoulder, sneaking a peek at her through the soft glow of the kitchen window.

Jesus. The sight of her still made his heart race, even after all these years. She was still the sexiest, most gorgeous thing he'd ever set eyes on, and he looked forward to the coming years with a keen, hungry anticipation. He'd never get enough of the woman who had brought so much love and happiness to his life. Not ever. He'd been blessed, and he was a man who was never going to forget it.

Caleb groaned beside him, catching his pop's lovesick look out of the corner of his jade green eyes. "Christ, Dad, sometimes it's embarrassing how you look at Mom. You guys have been married twenty-two years now. Enough already, old man."

Jake punched him in the shoulder, knocking the cocky twenty-one year old off the swing. "Watch it, pup. I may be fifty, but I can still take you."

Caleb snorted, as cocky and arrogant as Jake had been at that age. Hell, Taylor told him he was still a cocky bastard, but she loved him in spite of it. And she always loved him well, he thought with a wicked smile.

"It's just not natural. That's all. None of my friend's parents go around sneaking off for quickies and lookin' all lust-crazed," Caleb teased, his green eyes dark and mischievous.

"Must have married the wrong person, then," Jake drawled, taking a long swallow of his ice-cold beer. A gentle breeze stirred the surface of the water, blowing his black hair that held only a touch of gray at the temples. "Don't ever get married till you're ready, Caleb. When it's the right woman, you'll know, and you won't be able to keep your eyes or your hands off of her. And not just for a week or a month, son, but for a lifetime."

Caleb scratched his dark blue T-shirt covered chest, wincing at the thought of tying himself to one woman forever. "God help me," the young man muttered, sounding completely appalled. "What if it's in the blood?" He looked over his wide shoulders, catching a look at his mom through the same kitchen window, pondering at the strange connection his parents shared. "Damn," he swore softly, "I might get struck as hard as you."

Jake's deep laugh filled the soft silence of the garden. "You'll be a lucky bastard if you do. Trust me."

His son looked back at him, not with the eyes of a boy, but with the sudden insight of a man. Jake's heart twisted with pride.

"Is it worth it?" Caleb asked.

"It's worth anything in the world, Cale. Anything in the world."

The following is available in eBook from
Ellora's Cave Publishing, Inc.

www.ellorascave.com

MAGICK MEN:
A SHOT OF MAGICK

Preview

MAGICK MEN: A SHOT OF MAGICK

At six-five, he was tall and mean and muscle-honed from all the long, grueling hours he spent training other *Magicks* — Warlocks and Witches — in the arts of combat and self-defense. He had thick, reddish brown hair that he normally kept trimmed much shorter than his outrageous cousins, light green eyes, and golden skin. He was well dressed, always in control of his strong, passionate emotions, and wealthy enough to afford any luxury he wanted, from houses to cars to women. Though sex was one thing he'd never had to pay for.

He'd always had a look of danger, but now that look took on a more sinister character. His hair was longer, shaggy around the strong bones of his face, jaw dark with auburn stubble, big body wrapped up in ragged jeans, a black T-shirt, and big black boots as he left his house to pace the early, fog-filled streets of Edinburgh.

He looked like the kind of man you wouldn't want to meet in a dark alley, and he felt like one as well. And to be honest, he didn't know how much more of this he could take.

You'll take as much as you have to, man, his Warrior's pride warned. *Because you canna let those blasted fools win. Not this time! You've pledged them your bloody loyalty, but they havenna any claim on your cock!*

Yeah, well, too bad the governing High Council of Magicks — made up of his five outrageous uncles — thought otherwise.

They'd put a bloody curse on him, the well-meaning fools. One that changed his women into fucking animals every time he shot his blasted load. And the only way around it was to find his *bith-bhuan gra* — his soul mate.

His uncles, it seemed, had taken it upon themselves to ensure that he stopped sowing wild oats and began planting a few instead.

In the belly of the right woman, of course.

It was intolerable. He was so full of sexual frustration his skin felt like it was about to burst. Hot, tight, and disturbingly prickly, like an itch beneath the surface that remained just beyond his reach. He'd tried alleviating the painful pressure on his balls himself, taking matters into his own big hands, but ended up putting his fist through his shower wall when he'd been unable to bring release.

That was apparently yet another one of the Council's twisted concoctions. According to their sadistic curse, he could only achieve an orgasm with a woman. And if he didn't want to find himself shooting his cursed load of magic in front of another friggin' furry pet, he had to find the true woman — whatever the hell that meant.

He'd found *her* three weeks ago, when he was on a walk just like this one. And he'd dreamed of her each night since.

There was only one problem.

Well, one on top of the fact that his uncles had plagued him with a freaking curse on his cock and he couldn't screw without shooting a load of magic that turned his women into angry animals, leaving them craving a piece of his ass to chew on.

His balls were blue, his time was running out, and instead of searching for the true *Cailleach*—his *bith-bhuan gra*—he'd become obsessed with *her*. She was goddamn fascinating, beautiful and intelligent and spirited as hell. So different from any woman he'd ever known before.

There was just that one minor, somewhat unfortunate detail.

The woman who haunted his sleep and every waking hour was not a *Magick*.

She was not of his kind.

No, the woman of his dreams was a fucking mortal.

About the author:

Rhyannon Byrd is the wife of a Brit, lucky mother of two amazing children, and maid to a precocious beagle named Misha. In her seven years of marriage, she's moved from California to England, and then back to California again (they forgot to tell her there's no central heating in houses built 200 years ago) and finally to Florida, where she doesn't have to worry about it getting cold. It's been an exhausting existence, but in the past year she's somehow managed to find the time to put pen to paper— or fingers to keyboard—and give life to the stories and characters she loves. That is, when she's not threatening to kill her computer!

She graduated magna cum laude with a degree in Literature and Writing Studies, and while at school she spent most of her time writing papers on the psychoanalysis of medieval lit. Hmm...hardly a useful tool in modern day America, but hey, at least it taught her how to write. Now her days (and let's face it, most nights) are filled with creating the erotic love stories she enjoys most; those about strong alpha heroes and the fascinating women who capture their hearts, keeping all that wicked wildness for their own. When not writing, Rhyannon loves watching football and F1 racing, reading, painting, and traveling—but most of all she loves her crazy, supportive, hellion-filled family.

Please visit Rhyannon's website at www.rhyannonbyrd.com, and contact her at rhyannon@rhyannonbyrd.com. She loves to hear from readers.

Rhyannon welcomes mail from readers. You can write to her c/o Ellora's Cave Publishing at 1337 Commerce Drive, Suite 13, Stow OH 44224.

Also by Rhyannon Byrd:

Why an electronic book?

We live in the Information Age—an exciting time in the history of human civilization in which technology rules supreme and continues to progress in leaps and bounds every minute of every hour of every day. For a multitude of reasons, more and more avid literary fans are opting to purchase e-books instead of paperbacks. The question to those not yet initiated to the world of electronic reading is simply: *why?*

1. *Price.* An electronic title at Ellora's Cave Publishing runs anywhere from 40-75% less than the cover price of the <u>exact same title</u> in paperback format. Why? Cold mathematics. It is less expensive to publish an e-book than it is to publish a paperback, so the savings are passed along to the consumer.

2. *Space.* Running out of room to house your paperback books? That is one worry you will never have with electronic novels. For a low one-time cost, you can purchase a handheld computer designed specifically for e-reading purposes. Many e-readers are larger than the average handheld, giving you plenty of screen room. Better yet, hundreds of titles can be stored within your new library—a single microchip. (Please note that Ellora's Cave does not endorse any specific brands. You can check our website at www.ellorascave.com for customer

recommendations we make available to new consumers.)

3. *Mobility.* Because your new library now consists of only a microchip, your entire cache of books can be taken with you wherever you go.

4. *Personal preferences are accounted for.* Are the words you are currently reading too small? Too large? Too…**ANNOYING**? Paperback books cannot be modified according to personal preferences, but e-books can.

5. *Innovation.* The way you read a book is not the only advancement the Information Age has gifted the literary community with. There is also the factor of what you can read. Ellora's Cave Publishing will be introducing a new line of interactive titles that are available in e-book format only.

6. *Instant gratification.* Is it the middle of the night and all the bookstores are closed? Are you tired of waiting days—sometimes weeks—for online and offline bookstores to ship the novels you bought? Ellora's Cave Publishing sells instantaneous downloads 24 hours a day, 7 days a week, 365 days a year. Our e-book delivery system is 100% automated, meaning your order is filled as soon as you pay for it.

Those are a few of the top reasons why electronic novels are displacing paperbacks for many an avid reader. As always, Ellora's Cave Publishing welcomes your questions and comments. We invite you to email us at service@ellorascave.com or write to us directly at: 1337 Commerce Drive, Suite 13, Stow OH 44224.

Printed in the United States
21428LVS00002B/1-63